PICKLES

CLOWN~CUNT

For

By Gregor Cole

Gregor

PUBLISHER'S NOTE.

MorbidbookS is a grotesque Bizarro ballet where the most profane things occur. An impious and perverse dwelling of dark revulsion. A cozy cottage where torture porn and brutal bible tales are devised. A quiet place to relax and spin tales of depravity and wickedness. A halfway house for the disturbed where rules no longer apply. A safe haven for deviant serial killers to hatch their wretched schemes. Bring your pets. The tasty ones are always welcome.

HTTPS://WWW.MORBIDBOOKS.WORDPRESS.COM

ONE

CHRIS HAD LOCKED THE BACK DOOR. He checked all the sockets in the kitchen. They were all switched off. Chris made sure there was some food in the bowl for the cat.

He stood at the bottom of the stairs and double checked the television in the front room was off by looking for the red LED at the bottom of the screen. It was off. A huge weight lifted.

"Can't go wasting energy," He nodded to himself as he climbed the stairs. He was pleased as punch knowing he had a low carbon footprint.

Then began his nightly bathroom routine: cleaning his teeth with Pure Glisten, his favourite mild whitening tooth paste. Next he washed his face with Ned Barker's Tool Shed masculine face scrub. He clipped away the odd stray nasal hair with his Simmons's fuzz-be-gone electric waterproof nostril trimmer. Applying a thin layer of Manshine night time moisturiser for men, had made his facial tissue tingle delightfully.

He looked into the mirror and smiled, "There, all done." Chris took his final piss of the day. He flushed, switched off the light and made his way to the bedroom.

He flicked on the 24 hour news with the remote and threw it on to the double king-size bed, before slipping into his bespoke paisley night bottoms.

The sheets were crisp and clean and as he got in it felt like liquid on his tired skin. Chris wriggled into the double thick temper-foam mattress and took a book from the side table, Fifty Flavours of Vanilla Bean Sex.

He thumbed the pages, the mediocre soft-core pornography drew too heavy and he was asleep with the book on his belly. The television continued to inform the sleeping man about some war in the Middle East.

Chris began to snore. An inch of drool hung like a slick comma from his bottom lip.

It was the sound of the cat flap on the kitchen door slapping shut that stirred Chris from his slumber. Groggy, he scooped away the sheets sending the trash paperback to the floor.

Chris leaned over to reclaim the dropped book only to brush an oversized shoe with his hand.

At first he thought he was dreaming. There could be no other reason for a giant shoe being there. His hand padded the ground. The only illumination was the gloom from the television light. It was in that he clarified that he was indeed seeing two big shoes that shouldn't have been there.

Chris was sure he was awake.

He rubbed his eyes. Chris sat up only to face the silhouettes of several figures standing in his bedroom. They were smiling as they stared at him.

In a panic he scrambled for the bedside lamp and was sent into a shiver as the light lit a naked female clown. She was standing in the shoes by the side of his bed.

There were seven of them in all; seven naked clown women standing there, watching him rise groggily from sleep.

The clown girl closest to the bed jumped on him, her naked pussy rubbing against his belly as she straddled him. She grabbed his wrists. The other clown women fell on to the bed armed with long thin balloons. They tied them to his feet and arms, thus lashing him to the bed posts.

There was a squeak of rubber as he struggled. It put his teeth on edge and the bonds were way too tight. God, he'd hated balloons. The feel of them, the noise they made when they were blown up but most of all the anticipation of them popping.

Gregor

He was helpless as the clown girls backed away from the bed to reveal a tiny man dressed in a little red army coat and a wee top hat standing in the middle of the room.

"Mr Doyle, I would like to congratulate you on winning our once in a lifetime amazing competition." The little man danced from foot to foot. "We are here to give you you're prize."

"What fucking competition? What the fuck are you fucking freaks babbling about?" Chris spat at the little fellow. "Who are you?"

"How very rude of me Mr Doyle, my name is Ring Master Thumtumbulous and these are my Funny Girls." The little man tipped his hat and waved an arm of presentation toward the face-painted naked women around him. Each struck a sexy pose as his hand went down the line.

"GET THE FUCK OUT OF MY HOUSE!" Chris couldn't contain his panicked anger.

"No, no, no Mr Doyle, you are a winner." The little ring master circled the bed, barely able to see over the mattress. "You were handed a flyer outside the super market concerning our circus and you called the woman that gave it to you... oh, what was it again?" He held his chin in a little display of sarcasm.

One of the clown girls leaned in, "I believe he called her a *freak* Ring Master."

"That was it, a freak!" The little man nodded.

"You are freaks, you retarded fucking midget!" Chris struggled to free himself from the balloons squeaking clutches, but it came to nothing.

"Winnet, Bella, gag the man. I don't want to hear any more of his filth."

The girls dived on to the bed, their tits bouncing in Chris's face. In other circumstances he may we have enjoyed the experience but you just know it's going downhill from here.

Cole

The girls forced his mouth open and put in a plastic dental guard, wedging his jaw open. One of the girls pulled a deflated balloon from her neatly shaved pussy. She wore a red clown wig but her pussy was crowned with a tiny blond Mohawk.

He was pinned to the bed by the clown girl in a green wig. The red wigged girl dunked the wet balloon into Chris's prone mouth. She then leaned in almost to kiss him and with one big breath, she blew the balloon up in his maw.

Chris gagged as the inflatable tickled the back of his throat. His stomach turned with the sound and feel of it rubbing his teeth. With the balloon inflated the girls rubbed their tits in his face and stuck their tongues into each other's mouths and giggled.

"That's enough girls, as you were." The little ring master clapped his hands and the two clowns hopped off the bed with a little wiggle of their arses. "Are you ready for you prize, Mr Doyle?"

From behind the rubber he tried to shout 'GO FUCK YOURSELF' but it came out as a weird buzzing hum.

"Good." The little man took a back step. "Girls, show Mr Doyle what he's won!"

Every girl started pulling handfuls of flat balloons from inside themselves, each handful wet with juices from pussy and arse.

"Mr   Doyle,"   the   little   man   danced   again, "CONGRATULATIONS!"

The Funny Girls enveloped the bed in a wave of wet pussy and squeaking rubber.

T W O

THE LAST LUMP OF CRYSTALLISED CHEMICAL crackled away inside the burnt up light bulb.

Fingers covered with soot clung to the makeshift pipe as his painted lips sucked out the smoke. The flame from the trembling disposable lighter caught the glitter in his blue afro. His eyes sunk into the smudged grease paint like piss holes in the snow.

Pickles the Clown slumped back into his chair as the smoke worked its magic in his lungs.

The chemical was being absorbed like a sponge by his near to kaput alveolar membrane. It then rushed into the pulmonary capillaries and into his blood stream. The sweet steam hurried towards his brain adding yet another tiny black spot of damage to his grey matter.

His eyes rolled up into his head as his body shivered from the first wave of intoxication and the world around him flushed away.

Pickles was buzzing from his big toe to his last hair follicle. A sensation of euphoric rapture ensued. It was if his entire body was being licked by a million amateur porn starlets. His limp penis twitched with a pulse of stimuli from the drug signalling his return to reality and his eyes rolled back into the real world. The buzz passed as quickly as it had come leaving Pickles a little disorientated but still high as shit. Pickles had voided his bladder into his sweatpants. "Aw, fuck it!"

He got up dizzy with the effects of the junk he had bought from Dominic the pimp earlier that morning and staggered towards the bathroom to fetch a towel. He pulled down the soaked sweatpants and threw them onto a heap of unwashed laundry.

He washed his dick and his inner thighs in the sink with cold water then stared off into the mirror. The grotty bathroom looked like a stained glass window behind his gaunt made-up face as the residual effect of the drug changed his visual perception.

He walked back out into the hallway; he would need cigarettes and some coffee, maybe a hit or two of sleeping tablets. The chemical in his blood would wear off soon enough and the comedown was hard.

Pickles then stepped bare foot into a pile of cold cat shit.

He owned a cat; it was in the flat somewhere. He could hear it moving around under the piles of dirty cloths and ripped up porn at night. It had made the hallway stink of piss. Pickles would get through a lot of incense.

He'd leave a bowl of food down for it every now and then and when he would return to check it was always empty... unless he had rats in there and they had eaten the cat's corpse.

Pickles returned to the sink to wash the turd from between his toes when he heard some post get jammed into his letter box. Through the meshed glass of his front door he heard the postman call him a fucking junky. This always pissed Pickles off.

"Fucking junky?" he posed aloud, thinking hard enough to crease the corpse paint on his forehead. "You simple civil servant," Pickles vented, "I'm a CUNT, motherfucker. One hundred percent."

One time he had caught his postman urinating in his doorway. Looking back he should have reported him but didn't as he had been awake for three days and had lost the use of coherent speech. He later got high and forgot about the whole thing and could only really recall it in a series of almost surreal flashbacks.

Pickles would often forget things in that way.

Maybe it is *all the fucking junk I do,* he considered whilst cleaning the cat shite from his crusty heel.

With his newly cleaned foot he padded across the laminate floor of the hall, avoiding the shit this time to where the crumpled mail lay on the door mat. He stooped to pick it up. A task made all the more difficult with all the narcotics messing with his depth perception.

A stack of bills, companies telling him that they would be taking him to court if he didn't pay up some sort of fee. He had these every day; he didn't even need to open them to tell what they were.

Gregor

"Bills, bills, occupant, bills, and more bi- ... *ohfuckme...* "

His narcotic filled blood froze when his eyes fell on an envelope he recognised. It was one of fine parchment with a single word scrawled on it in fancy black calligraphy; there was no post mark and no stamp. It read *urgent.*

This letter was posted by hand. They were sending for him again and it meant for trouble. It wasn't to be ignored. The consequences were unthinkable.

Pickles staggered back into the front room and slumped onto his sofa. He placed the letter on the cluttered coffee table in front of him and searched for his cigarettes. His fingers shaking, he pulled one from the roughed up box and after a few tries, Pickles lit it with his trusty disposable.

He glared down at the foreboding correspondence.

One the one hand he'd open it, read it, obey the commands therein and get himself into some fine jam. On the other hand he could ignore it and spend the rest of his life looking over his shoulder and submerging himself even that much deeper in the clown underground.

The thought made him shudder.

He drew on his cigarette deeply and snatched up the letter. It was like a plaster on a tender area; if he opened it slowly it would only hurt more.

Pickles tore at the flap and pulled free the letter from inside. The paper was fine and smelt of bubble gum with a water mark resembling a circus big top.

He drew once more on the cigarette, blowing the smoke from his nostrils at the letter. His stomach knotted as he read the letter aloud:

Pickles,

You are here by summoned to stand before Il Consigliore Pagliaccio. Your expertise in certain fields is need in a matter of great urgency. The time and place will be made known to you by one of our agents in due course.

Signed,
Patch Theobald,
High Councillor.

Pickles shook his head.

I am fucked.

He dropped the letter to the floor at his feet and stubbed the cigarette into an overflowing ashtray on the table. He flopped back into the sofa and rubbed his hands across his face smudging his makeup further.

A meeting with the High Council of Clowns was the last thing he needed.

Fucked.

THREE

GIBBON WAS TAKING FIVE.

He'd been doing his job for so long now that the shine had worn off a little. Most people thought filming pornography was a dream job but that couldn't be further from the truth. Especially now that the circumstances had changed.

It had started out great, sure, working with pretty girls and professional studs for the bigger producers. He had worked on some of the best properties and private lots in the business but then the recession hit and hit hard. All but three of the big producers shut down or went to internet only and the money dried up quicker than an aged porn star after the menopause.

Gibbo was lucky; he had caught a break working for this guy that sold to the privet markets. Gibbo copped a sweet deal shooting his own POV movies. He got to bang loads of prostitutes in motels while filming it all with a handheld camera.

Then the strange orders came through like play-rape, beatings, humiliation, piss and shit fun. If it wasn't for the coke habit and medication bills for all the STD's he'd developed over the last two years he would have turned it all down.

But alas, someone has to do the dirty work.

He propped himself up against a self-store container. Gibbo absently scratched his beard to the sounds of two speed freaks roughly stuffing a baseball bat into the anus of a crack head. He heard it all through the thin panelling. Wish he couldn't, but the walls were so thin he could even hear the dudes when they spat in her mouth.

The sound of a punch to the crack whore's stomach made him gag a little as he smoked and scratched.

By the time the rhythmical slapping of nutsack against wet arsehole started he was sitting in his car going through the glove box. Gibbo was looking for his .38 pistol.

Sweat rolled down his forehead and he pulled his shoulder length hair back into a little nub on the back of his head.

He turned on the radio. Neil Diamond. He turned off the radio.

Gibbon had lost count the amount of times he had put that barrel into his mouth and tickled the trigger He'd never managed to pluck up the courage to squeeze. Gibbo often wanted something to startle him so he would accidently blow the back of his skull all over the interior of his shit box Volvo.

The gun had a strange taste, like off milk. Gibbo put that down to the amount of dried saliva that was inside the barrel. He had never cleaned the thing and only ever fired it once at a road sign to see if it worked.

The kick of it gave him a start and because he was a little high he nearly shit in his pants from the sound. He had left it in his car ever since but every now and then he would sit there, with it in his mouth, waiting for someone to knock on the window out of the blue.

Gibbo pulled it free from his lips; a string of drool formed a bridge from his bottom lip to the raised sight in the barrel. He peered down the black hole of the gun and wondered what it would look like if it went off in his face.

Would he feel it? Wondered Gibbon, and would he even give a fuck?

He slumped over the searing wheel face down with his arms flopped over the dash, the drool now dribbling from his mouth down to the sticky mat in the foot well. He let it happen. He had no shame by this point.

He wondered whether the speed freaks had killed the crack whore. He wondered if he would care if they had.

The sound of someone knocking on his passenger window caused him to jump. He clenched his hands instinctively and the .38 spat a lump of hot lead through his windscreen, accompanied by a deafening clap.

In a panic he screamed and dropped the gun. It went off again sending a bullet into the engine block of the car and again with an ear splitting bang. He grabbed for the door and fell out onto the gravel. The person that had knocked on the window was cowering on the other side of the colour miss-matched vehicle.

"For fuck sake, Gibbo, what the fuck was that?"

Gibbo recognised the voice through the ringing in his ears. It was Ruby, one of the girls he worked with. She specialised in oversized insertions and her gimmick was clown make-up. Gibbo had shot a lot of clown porn.

Almost too much.

Her head popped up over the roof of the car. Ruby's purple hair pulled up into a pineapple. Her face was white with perfect red circles on her cheeks. One eye painted with a green diamond, the other a blue triangle. The thick red of her lips looked like her head was split in two.

"You're not going to try and kill me are you?" She waved to Gibbon who just stared up at the sky.

"No, you're okay; I was just having a meditative moment, honey." He rolled over and crawled his way over to the car and used it to climb to his feet, "Nothing to worry about, just one of those days." Ruby hopped around the car to help him dust down.

The door of the container was flung open and one of the speed freaks stuck his head out to see what the commotion was. Gibbo waved him away like a bad smell and the door soon slammed shut in a huff.

How dare they interrupt their crack whore cunt whipping?

"Fucking junkies," Ruby shook her head, "can't fucking stand those pricks, get off hurting girls. They'd kill 'em if they thought they could."

"Yeah, but it pays the bills, honey." Gibbon reached into the car and shoved the pistol back into the glove box. "I just let them get on with it now. What they do is totally down to them."

"But they are still fucking sick."

"Tell me about it. I have the lovely job of editing four different cameras worth of their rape footage later on today, but only after I have the pleasure of your company, honey."

"Aw, thank you Gibbo, you make it sound so nice."

"Yeah, I'm a real sweetheart." He took a cigarette from his shirt pocket and scratched at his thick beard again. "Anyhow, those pricks will be done in a minute then we can set up."

As Ruby was about to give the big lunk a huge hug a white van with fat tyres and wide arches rolled up on the gravel drive. Its big V8 engine thumped as the vehicle came sliding to a stop on the loose surface, kicking up a cloud of dust as it did so.

The windscreen was tinted but they could still make out a figure; one with a big blue afro and mirrored aviator sunglasses. Grindcore blasted out from inside the tank-like van sending vibrations through the metal panels. It caused something to vibrate at the same frequency of the fat riffs and a crack in the window buzzed with the bass line.

The van stopped and the driver jumped down from his high driving position. He wore cut-down combat shorts, a black and white pair of high-tops and a t-shirt with *100% CUNT* on the front in big white letters.

They both recognised who it was straight away. It was Pickles.

Fuck.

He was outside on a weekday.

He wasn't expected and he wasn't here to pick up drugs.

That meant trouble.

Fucked.

FOUR

"SO WHAT BRINGS YOU HERE, GOOD BUDDY?" Gibbo had thrown out the stars of his last movie and finished wiping the secretions from the furniture. The odour of crack smoke and anal sex still lingered no matter how much lavender air freshener he sprayed.

"Well, I've come for Ruby." Pickles expression was dour.

"I ain't going anywhere, I have a scene to shoot then I'm getting my nails done." Ruby sat with on a beanbag in the corner of the coverted container. Her arms were crossed like a petulant child

"Fuck your nails, bitch," Pickles was not happy at the reply and glared through his aviators at the sulking girl. "I've been called in to see the council."

Gregor

The room was quiet for a moment, like Gibbo's gun had gone off by accident again. It was Gibbo that broke the silence.

"That can't be anything good."

"No, it can't." Pickles was still staring at Ruby. "So I'm going to need some help."

"I'm not going." Ruby huffed.

"I'm not asking."

"Good."

Pickles leaned in a little closer to where Ruby was sulking. "I'm fucking telling."

Ruby looked almost shocked at the audacity of the dirty junky fuck. Who was he to bark orders, after all jams she had got him out of.

"A fucking washed up clown telling me what to do, who the fuck do you think…"

"I'm the guy that stopped Dingo Jack from raping your arse, beating you and leaving you dead in my place, you ungrateful whore." Pickles flopped back into his seat, he had played his hand.

"You can't bring that up." Rube looked like she might cry.

"I can and I have."

"That's dark, Pickles man, you know she's grateful for that, we all are." Gibbo was almost on the verge of smashing the clowns face in but knew if the council was calling it was for a good reason.

"Why do they want you in, or is it the usual hush-hush operation?"

"Don't know, don't care, usual bullshit, information or some sort of favour, but I'm going to need support." Pickles took off his sun glasses. His blood-shot eyes were ringed with black make-up. "I'm in a bad way and need a little help… mentally."

"You do look messed up." Ruby got to her feet, her face instantly change to one of gloating joy. "Hitting that glass dick a little too hard, eh?"

"Fuck you, cum bucket." Pickles rubbed at his eyes, letting the lies roll off his tongue. "Nothing I haven't been through before."

"Really? Because you look fucked to me."

"Ruby, the man's going through some shit, we've all been there." Gibbo pulled up a chair in front of Pickles. "Now when you say mental, what level are we talking?"

"Oh, the normal shit: the fear, visual interference, scared of the outside world, mild uncontrollable hallucinations. You know, nothing too bad but enough to worry."

"So back-up is needed then." Gibbo scratched at his beard again and turned to Ruby. "I think you might give the guy a break, honey."

"I dunno, this guy is just trouble and I don't trust him."

"Look you can either help me out or I can explain to the council that I turned to a sister for help and she turned me down, even out in the sticks they can make it hard for you to get work." Pickles wiped the sweat from his brow. "The rumour of venereal disease in the ear of the right people and they'll drop you quicker than a burning turd. You'll have to play the game for real. There'll be no more picking and choosing, just like this chump." He threw a thumb at Gibbo who nodded woefully.

"He's right, honey. The council could shut you done real fast, you'll end up like that crack head bitch getting destroyed for food stamps and rock hits."

Ruby's face dropped as the realisation that they were right set in. She was cute but a few months on the perv circuit would sort that out. A few black eyes, the occasional broken finger and a couple of swift kicks in the crotch wouldn't help her one bit and the mere sniff of VD would instantly put her in the junky category. Fair game. Open season. All the slime would be after her then.

The girls that worked in those circles never lasted too long. They usually turned to the junk. Or else they'd end up being found

Gregor

under a plastic sheet somewhere by old folks walking their four-legged shit machine.

She knew what side her bread was buttered.

"So if I help you this one time does that mean you'll owe me a pretty big favour?"

"Yeah, I guess so. That's if I last long enough to owe you." Pickles reluctantly nodded. "So you'll help?"

"Any favour, no matter how big?" Ruby was getting anxious.

"What, like caving in a rapist's skull for you?"

"Fuck sake, Pickles." Gibbo leaned back in his chair.

"You're never letting that go are you?" Ruby was still not happy that he couldn't let it go.

"All I'm saying is I will owe you to the point of putting someone in a wheelchair for life...again!"

Gibbo looked worried and stared at Ruby when he asked. "So when's all this going down, when's the meet?"

"Dunno, they said I will be approached by an agent, whatever that means."

"Well you better get your shit together then." Gibbo got up and started to tinker with a large VHS camera on a tripod. "And you young lady have a scene to shoot, so if you don't mind Pickles, I don't care if you stay I just don't want you in the way."

Pickles did as he was told and plonked himself down on the beanbag in the corner as Gibbo set up for the shoot. Pickles was nearly blinded by the redhead lamp Gibbo switched on that was attached to the celling of the container. It burnt at his retinas like branding irons and he was forced to put his sunglasses back on.

Ruby meanwhile stripped down to her birthday suit and tied her hair up. She then rifled through her bag of props. Both men's jaws dropped as she produced an inflatable rubber chicken from the duffle bag.

She made her way to a grotty little mattress propped up on a stack of shipping pallets. Ruby hopped up on to the makeshift bed and spread her legs wide exposing her thin lipped pussy to the camera.

"Gibbo, be a love and get some lube from my bag. I might need it for my arse."

Class, Pickles thought. *All class.*

FIVE

A MONTH'S WORTH OF SEMEN sat in the large sample jar at the back of the fridge. It was just next to the big slice of watermelon wrapped in cling film and the opened tin of baked beans.

The beans were on the turn.

The jar was as good as alone when the dark of the sealed fridge was suddenly awash with brilliant light. A giant hand reached in for it. If the jar had have been sentient it would have trembled with fear at the sight on the huge digits coming towards it.

But it was just a jar full of cum.

Five times a day. Every day for thirty days he had spunked into that jar and all in the name of high art. He had saved enough to get at least three paintings done.

Dominic and done this every three months for the last two years living on a diet of cabbage soup, lettuce and fruit, downing pint after pint of water to keep himself hydrated. The higher the hydration the bigger the loads he could chuck into the cup.

He would use the spunk as paint onto black cloth then the artist then took some photographs of the paintings whilst lit with ultra-violet bulbs.

He had gotten the idea from one of those crap reality shows where some inspectors poked around hotels to see how clean they were. Dominic was fascinated with how dried seamen looked under black light. The way it glowed had him captivated. He had found his medium and it was going to make him infamous.

Dominic had experimented with several bodily fluids over the years in various mediums. He had held an exhibition where he made sculpture from his own shit. The highlight was a piece called Pepper Pot. The display was a huge pillar of turd with a big pink -P- wedged into it.

To say the exhibition didn't go down well was an understatement.

He had also worked with spit, setting up a high speed camera. When he had the flu he photographed himself hocking up phlegm, spitting it across a black background. The pictures caused some controversy as he was naked in every one and in some of the longer shots, clearly aroused. His college tutors were not amused.

Dominic was an artist, what did they know?

Then there was his sick phase, similar to Picasso's 'blue' period but with vomit. This was more of a conceptual phase working with cheap super8 cameras. He would go out and gorge himself with beer and kebabs then film himself throwing up in various places.

He was arrested after vomiting onto a bus stop full of people from a multi-story car park after stuffing himself with a curry and eight pints of stout. In the aftermath he was forced to pay for the counselling one woman had to receive after seeing her child in its pushchair get smothered buy a javelin of barf.

The child survived.

Dominic opened the spunk jar and was hit with the aroma of the sea. He couldn't resist the urge to touch it and make little peaks with the chilled jizum like on a lemon meringue pie with the tip of his finger.

He did however resist the temptation to pop the tip of his finger in his maw and give it a taste.

With his studio set for his master work The Spunkening. It was on the verge of completion. A vast expanse of black cloth was laid out on the floor and a black light tube hummed away overhead.

But it was the way he applied the semen to the canvas that made this work extra-special. He'd taken a giant rubber strap-on dick and modified it with a turkey baster. The artist was going to cum all over the black sheet. Dominic was more excited than he had been in years as he stripped down to just his socks and strapped the dildo on.

This was going to be a masterpiece.

He turned off the lights and switched on the UV bulb. His skin took on a strange green shade. All the little scars and blemishes on his arms stood out in neon purple.

Dominic had set up a series of security cameras around the room to capture the moment. With a little tinkering he could cut and paste the footage to some heavy industrial music and use it as a video installation. It was going to be the centre point of the exhibition.

He rubbed the rubber cock in his left hand as if it were his own and pressed the button on a key ring remote control clipped to the strap-on. The cameras were rolling and Dominic eyed his first shot of baby gravy.

It was then the phone in the next room started to ring, "For fuck sake!"

The lights went on, the bulb went off and he stormed out of the studio pressing the remote to the cameras.

"Whoever this is better giving me money, or head or both." He snatched up the receiver, the rubber dick still bobbing between his legs, "Who the fuck is this?"

"Dominic Bench, listen very carefully," the man's voice on the other end sounded like he had been smoking gravel, "I will say this only once."

Gregor

THE INFLATED RUBBER CHICKEN popped out of her arsehole followed by a squelch of lube and anal mucus as her sphincter started to close.

Gibbo was closing in on Ruby's butt with the camera in hand to capture the anal gape as Pickles went through the ashtray looking for roaches to smoke in the corner of the room. The rubber chicken was slowly deflating on the floor with a weak, long farting sound as the air escaped from the release valve.

Ruby looked over her shoulder and giggled wiggling her arse in the air. She winked at the camera and poked her tongue out.

How could someone so cute do something so vile? Pickles wondered. He didn't look up once during the recording. He was too busy trying to feel like a human. Too difficult when a girl is sodomising herself with a clown prop.

"And that as they say," Gibbo stopped the camera, "is a wrap."

Ruby flopped over on to her side. Her face went from childishly playful to slightly pained and miserable.

"I think I've ripped something this time. It got really big in there at the end."

"You'll be okay, honey." Gibbo lit a cigarette. "It's not the biggest thing you've had up there. I know, remember the wine bottle?" A wide grin crossed his face and Pickles looked up from the ashtray for a moment with a raised eyebrow.

"That nearly broke me. I was convinced it was going to pop there for a moment." She rubbed her arsehole as she reminisced to sooth the pain a little. It didn't work, "Thought I might be shitting bits of yellow rubber for a week."

Gibbo laughed and started to pack the camera equipment away. "Well I think we are done for the day. Does anyone want to grab a beer, maybe something stronger?"

A noise started to emanate from Pickles crotch area. It took a moment for him to register it. It was his phone. The vibrate function was hard to gauge with his body still shaking with comedown. Gibbo and Ruby stared down at the clown who for a moment stared back through his mirrored shades.

"What?"

"Aren't you going to answer that?" Ruby scowled, folding her arms.

"Shit, yeah." Pickles fumbled for the device in his pocket, found it, pulled it out and looked at the screen. "It's Dominic."

Pickles answered to the sound of a man worried. "Hey, Pick, It's Dom."

The voice on the phone spluttered, "I've just had a call... from the council." Pickles froze up expecting bad news. "They asked me to tell you the meeting will be held in.... held in..." There was a pause that seemed to last an hour, *"Der Einsame Festung."*

Pickles dropped the phone and slumped back into the beanbag, running his hands through his blue afro as he groaned aloud.

"What's happening?" Gibbo looked worried.

"It's the meeting," Pickles mumbled. A lump formed in his throat and he let his head fall over the back of the beanbag.

"Well?" Ruby spat, "Where is it?"

"It's in the clown prison," Pickles stated flatly, "and I am proper fucked."

SIX

THE BLACK AND RED CIRCUS TENT SHIVERED from the storm. It passed over the clearing, deep in the woods and outside the small fishing village of Breen.

The village had been all but deserted years ago after an outbreak of fish-flu in the local waters that contaminated every

Gregor

catch the fishermen brought in. With no income the men packed up and took their families to fishing towns that didn't have rank waters.

With the area as good as forsaken the only folk left in the dead town were beach combers, squatters and smugglers.

All through the night tiny boats would land on the shore and men wearing head torches unload bundle after bundle of god knows what. Drugs, money, even people would be traded on the beaches of Breen.

There wasn't a policeman for miles and that's exactly why Thumtumbulous set up his camp there; way on out in the forest. They were miles away from civilisation.

The wind whipped up. The ropes came free from their moorings and lashed against the canvas walls. A gang of Hobo clowns bustled around in the high winds to re-stake the chaotic ropes. Then the hobos rounded up the last of the animals to take into the tent.

Everything was to be taken into the big top. Even the caravans were roped down and staked. Thumtumbulous stared out of the tiny round window in the door of his wagon to see one of the hobos running towards it.

"Mr Thumtumbulous, Mr Thumtumbulous, sir," The hobo was out of breath from his heavy chores. The little ring master opened the door of his squat caravan and let the painted man in.

"We have all the animals in, Mr Thumtumbulous, sir, and the tent is secure enough to weather a mightier storm than this, it's just..." The hobo removed his squashed top hat and run the brim in his gloved hands.

"It's just what, man? Speak up!" The little ring master hopped into his desk chair and took a vast chunk of cheese off his dinner plate, greedily stuffing it into his mouth.

"It's just we haven't seen the Funny Girls in a while. Hagar the strongman said he thought they were at the quicksand pit, with that girl they took from the town." The hobo looked at the floor and kicked his tatty shoes against the wooden wall of the caravan.

"WHAT?!" Thumtumbulous spat great lumps of the cheese across his desk. "Why haven't you gone out there to get them, man?"

"It's dark, sir. I didn't want to get lost in the woods with all the ghost and dead folk out there, sir."

"Tumbles, you fool, there are no ghosts. You shouldn't listen to those stupid campfire stories." The little man jumped down and snatched up his own top hat. "Come with me you coward, we shall fetch the girls together."

And with that the little man flung his caravan door open and marched out into the storm. The sad faced hobo followed still with his crushed hat in hand. His oversized shoes slapped down the wooden steps as he scurried after his master.

Rain had started to fall, light but enough to make the grass around the camp slippery and soft. Every droplet hit the trees and brought the woods alive with its hissing sound. The high wind shook the water from the leaves in sheets.

The hobo was a little nervous; he had heard all kinds of stories from the others in the camp. Ghosts, monsters and zombies crawling out from the soil to eat him were behind every tree, behind every bush.

But like his master had said, they were only stories. The others were taking advantage of him as he was a little slow.

The thick forest broke to another, smaller clearing lit with lanterns hanging from the trees. The Funny Girls were standing in a circle watching a large breasted naked woman struggling in a puddle of quicksand.

Two of the girls were masturbating. Another goaded the slowly sinking woman with a stick, holding it just out of reach. One took photos on an old Polaroid camera as the other three crouched at the edge of the quicksand. Their eyes were all lit up with glee as the woman's shoulders began to disappear under the slop.

"What the hell is going on, girls?" Thumtumbulous bounded over to the wallow. "A storm is coming; we have no time for frivolities."

One of the masturbating girls turned around still rubbing away at her wet slot. "But we just wanted to drown this milf."

"Darn fool harlots!" He raised a fist in anger and the girl fell back from the little man. "That milf was for the show. We don't have time to find another, now what's the man supposed to fuck?"

Thumtumbulous waved at the woman in the pit. "You'll have to stay there my dear." He turned to the girls now cowering behind their fallen sister. "The rest of you sluts get back to camp, Tumbles, make sure they get there and don't leave the tent." He switched back to the drowning woman. "I wish to watch the milf in the hole."

In a huff the girls wiggled off into the woods. The hobo hurried behind, shoeing them back to the safety of the big top.

With them all gone Thumtumbulous hopped up onto a fallen log by the quicksand pit .The little Ring Master watched as the last of the woman's neck was enveloped by the mire.

She struggled as the mug started to crawl its way up her face and over her nose. The more she writher under the surface the more the mud sucked at her, pulling her further down into the ground.

Ring Master whooped with delight as her forehead sank under leaving only the plated rope of her blond ponytail sticking out. And as she had, her hair slowly followed like a worm and disappeared with her under the liquid earth.

With his penis now rock hard from the spectacle Thumtumbulous went into the woods to masturbate up a tree. His little pecker spat a miniscule load of joy up the mottled bark.

He righted himself and made his way back to camp. He didn't trust the girls unsupervised. They could be up to all sorts of trouble and the last thing he wanted was a pack of pregnant killer clowns in his troop.

And besides they had a show to rehearse, but where would they find another woman at such short notice?

SEVEN

"THE FUCKING LONELY FORTRESS?" Ruby was more than agitated in as she rode shotgun in the white wide arched van. "You want me to go with you to the fucking clown prison."

"That's what I said, wasn't it?" Pickles was in no mood for such a dramatic outburst. "After all, it's me that has to meet with those fuckers in the council."

The night had turned ghastly. A storm was coming and rain had already started to spray down on the road making it almost impossible to see in sunglasses. Nothing was going to make Pickles took them off and he sat over the steering wheel close to the windscreen. The knuckles on both hands were white as he gripped the wheel.

Full of stress and come down he did his best to ignore the incensed Ruby.

She slammed her fist on the dash. "Are you even listening to me?"

Pickles had been so focused on the road and trying not to feel his comedown. He had zoned-out from the noise coming from her mouth. "No." He said squinting through his shades.

"I said, have you ever been to this place, do you even fucking know where it is?"

Pickles was starting to lose his cool. "No I have never been there and yes I know where it fucking is. Now shut the fuck up and let me concentrate." He turned on the radio to Stealer's Wheel's *I get*

Gregor

by. "Why don't you get in the back and sleep or something? It's going to be a long drive."

"Fuck you, you fucking two-bit sideshow cock sucker."

That was it.

Pickles slammed on the brakes sending Rudy hard into the dashboard. He turned and ripped of his shades, his eyes bloodshot to the point of infected and burning with anger.

"Listen to me, you fucking funnel-cunted dope-whore. You know full well I've had to do favours for these pricks before. And every time I've gone to see them I have wished I was never born. All I ask of you is to show me a little fucking support. Maybe supply a little back up if shit gets heavy. And if you don't like it, I bet I can always find some meth freak willing to finish off what that fat prick Dingo Jack. That sick fuck was going to destroy you like the pig you are!"

The van was still for a moment while Stealer's Wheel honked out of the speakers and the engine rattled the windows.

"Well..." Ruby climbed out of the foot well and sat back in the passenger seat. "That was a very articulate outburst." She stared at him, wanting to punch him in the teeth. "Can we go then or are we going to plot up here for the rest of the fucking night?" Calling her out like that wasn't going to do him any favours.

Pickles put the van in gear and stepped on the accelerator, his anger coming out in his driving with forced gear changes and aggressive over-revving of the engine.

"Look, I didn't want to bring it up..."

"Drop dead, prick."

Pickles was never going to let it go. He was never going to let her forget that if it wasn't for him that John would have done really bad things to her. She had been so scared and the relief she had felt when she heard him put the key in the front door was almost like an ecstasy high.

Cole

Pickles had caved Dingo Jack's head in with an ice bucket until both Jack's head and the bucket were flat. She could still hear the sound of every smash of the bucket on his skull. She could almost feel every splash of ice water and warm blood freckling her skin.

Ruby was grateful he had come home that day but she would never really let on. She had an image to uphold. Maybe one day she would thank him properly. Maybe when he was on his death bed dying from some drug related illness. Cancer or something would do just fine.

"I fucking love this song." Pickles put his sun glasses back on and pulled a packet of Royal lights from the glove box. He lit it with his silver lighter that had *100% CUNT* engraved on it. This self-assessment was kind of his slogan. It was little wonder he didn't get invited to more children's parties.

Ruby pulled her knees up to her chin and dragged a checked blanket from the seat. It smelt stale with the alluring aroma of oil but it was warm.

It was only a matter of time before she was sound asleep and dreaming of a white house with a white picket fence.

She could see herself through a window. She was wearing a red checked dress, her hair tied up with a bow and no make-up. Well, there was no clown make-up anyway.

The kitchen was clean. A baby sat in a high chair playing with alphabet blocks while she made gingerbread men. She stirred at the dough with a wooden spoon in a big ceramic bowl. There were birds singing in the garden and a man, Pickles was mowing the lawn and smoking a pipe. He wore a crisp white shirt under a brown sleeveless jumper and no clown make-up either.

Gregor

Pickles waved at Ruby through the window and Ruby responded by holding up the baby and waving the child's little arm back at him. "Wave to daddy," She smiled down at the baby.

Then a little blue bird landed on Pickles' shoulder tweeting a jaunty tune. He removed his pipe from his mouth and chortled at the creature then looked back at the house smiling. The baby giggled at the little bird as it flew away.

A perfect family scene.

Ruby was awoken sharply by Pickles opening the passenger door and shaking her by the shoulder. "Wake up, bitch, we have to get on a boat."

"Fuck, man, what the fuck?" Ruby rubbed the sleep from her eyes and peered out into the rain at a dark looking stretch of water and a boat waiting on a rickety jetty. The sky was just starting to get light but the storm hadn't given up yet.

Pickles was unpacking some gear from the side door of the van, throwing junk over his shoulder and stuffing things they might need into a dirty rucksack. He mumbled about the rain and having to get on a fucking boat in a storm.

Ruby yawned and stretched out. "Shit, man, did I just have the worst fucking nightmare or what?"

EIGHT

THE BOATMAN SPAT A FAT MOUTHFUL OF PHLEGM onto the deck inside the cramped cabin. It looked like a jellyfish. It glistened from the dull light via a bare bulb overhead as it flattened out on the dirty wooden flood. It made Ruby wretch.

Pickles was sleeping. He was stuffed into a corner with his rucksack and the blanket from the van. He was still wearing his shades, so the only way Ruby could tell he was asleep was from the drool running from the side of his partially open mouth, down his chin and onto his shirt.

It looked like he had suffered a stroke.

Maybe he had, maybe now was the time for Ruby to thank him for saving her. She was not that lucky. Pickles twitched in his slumber and wiped the saliva from his mouth, smearing it into his make-up.

This boat trip was getting a little too *spitty* for her liking.

The boat rocked violently from side to side in the stormy water. Its spot lamp only just cuts through the haze of the rain on the water. A bell on the top of the boat rang out every time the boat was bashed by another wave. The rhythmical chugging of the boat's engine reverberated through the rotten wood of the hull.

Ruby was feeling a little sea sick. It didn't help having the boatman clearing his lungs onto the floor every five minutes.

A radio by the boatman crackled and a voice buzzed through the airwaves. "Hugo, it that you out there?"

The boatman spat another jelly onto the floor and picked up the handset, "Yep, it's me. Can you see the lamp?"

"Just about. I'll put the jetty lights on, hold on."

Up ahead a string of dull lights blinked on, thus lighting up dark cliffs. These series of lights zig-zagged itself up the walls of the cliffs, way up high into the darkness of the stormy sky.

"Ya see em?" The voice on the radio crackled.

"Yep, be with you in a minute, out." He replaced the hand set and pulled on a lever to slow the boat to prevent it crashing into the rocks at the bottom of the black stone cliffs. "Wake him up, we're here."

The jetty stank of seaweed and burning tar. It was no more than a series of planks with a small shed at the shore. Metal cages protected the jetty lights on high poles. A miserable face peered from the shed window watching the party disembark.

Gregor

The man in the shed was lucky enough to catch Pickles vomiting into the black water off of the jetty. His detox was moving in to the nausea stage and it was not helped one bit by being woken on a boat in rocky seas.

"This place fucking reeks," Ruby noted. She was pulling at her jacket to try and get as much cover from the elements as she could. It was far too cold and wet for her silver hot pants and football socks. Her skin was raised with goose bumps and she rubbed her hands together briskly.

Pickles hadn't noticed the smell straight away but he was sick again when the oily air finally hit his taste buds. It flooded his nose with the stink of rotten fish.

"I don't know how long I can hold on before I pass the fuck out, Roobs." The clown was in a bad way. "I really don't want to spend that long here."

They had both heard the stories of the Clown Prison; The Lonely fortress was where they hid all the sick clowns that had brought shame onto the council. The paedophiles, the rapists, the porn stars driven mad by drugs. The clowns that had severe mental issues and turned to serial killing as a release from their ongoing psychosis were present in good numbers.

It was a place for the council to place all their embarrassments and it was full up.

Lots of fucked up clowns...

"You know who's meant to be in here, don't you?" Ruby was now visibly shivering.

"I have no idea, Father fucking Christmas?" Pickles was still trying to hold down the last of the fluid in his gullet.

"Johnny Palladuchi."

Pickles stomach knotted up into a ball and his blood ran cold. "The mime killer... shit. I thought the cops killed that fucking head case."

"Well that's the story." Ruby picked up the rucksack and followed the boatman to the shed with Pickles bringing up the rear. "I heard from this pimp that supplied man whores for the fight game a while back that specialised in... erm... well *specialist* stuff. He told me that they used Palladuchi in some underground snuff cage fighting thing. The kind where the fighting doesn't stop till one guy goes limp."

"Shit that's dark, are you trying to make me sick again?"

"Apparently he was top draw, killed over twenty guys with his bare hands in the ring until the pigs shut the operation down and the council found out he was still alive. Then they shipped his arse out here, tucked him away where no one would find him."

"So he's up in there punching the fuck out of a padded cell I suppose?" Pickles caught up and took the bag from Ruby. He rummaged in it for the jar of tranquilisers he knew she had. "Johnny Palladuchi was one of the world's greatest mimes, such a waste."

"Well that's what I heard."

The door to the shed opened and a hobo clown stepped out into the storm. The wind nearly drove his dirty shower cap clean off his head.

"Welcome to the island folks. I'm Capo and I'll take you to the top and on to the fortress." Under the sad face make-up he seemed quite jolly. "Hugo you can head back to the mainland, thanks."

"No problem, I'll radio when I hit land." The boatman sauntered back to his beat up boat. The little skiff began to chug away into the night until only the spot lamp could be seen in the gloom.

The hobo tuned to the other two clowns and pointed to the start of a stairway cut into the rocks of the cliff wall.

"Now if you'll follow me, people, we'll make our way up."

Gregor

<u>N I N E</u>

THERE'S THAT SQUEAK AGAIN. That sickening feeling of the thin rubber as is moved minutely against his teeth. It made Chris' eyes water and they blinked open into consciousness.

Even in his sleep he could smell dung. Now he knew why.

He was stooped down in a cage filled with mouldy straw and animal shit. A red and white striped canvas covered the outside of the cage but a little light from outside crept through. The space was humid to the point of overpowering especially being almost waist deep in shit and straw.

His hands were chained over his head to a bolt in the cage celling. The balloon was still inflated in his mouth. It itched at the back of his dry throat.

There was a pain too, a pain in his groin but deeper. It was on the inside of him, by his hip.

He was still wearing pyjama bottoms. As Chris stood he dropped the silk bed-time trousers until he saw what it was that was causing the pain. A bright yellow balloon knot was poking out of his bizarrely fat penis. He realised that the girls had stuffed his urethra with a modelling balloon and inflated it. The pain was the swollen inflatable stretching the walls of his bladder.

Chris started to cry a little.

One of the curtains over the cage started to twitch and he could make out the silhouette of people moving on the other side. He could hear girls giggling and his heart sank. If it wasn't for the obstruction in his dick he would have pissed himself with fear already.

The curtain started to slowly rise. Almost immediately he could see seven pairs of female legs, all wearing neon coloured legwarmers. Then further still to a selection of wiggling arses and a smorgasbord of pussies. Then up across toned stomachs and perky breast towards seven white faces and a range of coloured wigs.

The girls had come to see their guest.

"You don't look happy," A girl with a red bob wig giggled.

"We've come to cheers you up," Said another with pink pigtails.

"Would you like us to get rid of that nasty balloon?" A girl with a green ponytail pointed down towards his cock. "Bet you're just busting for a piss?"

Chris could do nothing but nod and sob a muffled moan past the colourful gag.

A girl with a red afro curled her finger, beckoning Chris to shuffle forward towards the bars of the cage. "Get your dick closer and I'll pull it out for you, baby."

He hopped closer to the waiting girl. Her hand snatched at his dick, grabbing it by the base. She squeezed hard sending the air inside towards the knot which bulged from the new pressure and the rest towards his bladder. The extra air stretched the piss bag even further. Chris let out a tiny squeaking fart from the added distention inside him.

"Oh you dirty thing! No wonder you're in that cage, you filthy animal," Came another voice from a girl in a yellow afro.

"Now let me get this free for you." The clown girl tugged at the knot hanging from the tip of his dick and made out like it wouldn't budge. Then she clicked her fingers and made a face like she had just had the greatest idea in the world. She started to rummage around in her nest of red nylon hair.

She pulled out a long silver pin and pointed it towards his bloated penis.

"Now this might make your eyes water a little," admitted the clown girl. She plunged the needle through his foreskin and into the meat at the tip of his cock. It ripped through the flesh with a little

Gregor

squirt of blood that was almost comical. The balloon popped inside his shaft.

The combination of excruciating pain and instant relief made Chris collapse backwards. The chains on his wrists prevented him from falling proper. And with a muffled scream, Chris let go of his swollen bladder and piss sprayed from his wounded dick like a sprinkler. He covered himself and the rest of the cage with bloody urine. The girls screamed with glee at the sight.

"Girls, please!" It was the dwarf from his room. "Leave the poor fool alone, he must remain unharmed for the show, you know. We've already had to make up for your earlier indiscretion, my dears, so no more of that!"

A bearded lady dressed as a gypsy and a bald muscle man dressed in leopard print pants struggled with a woman. Her hands were secured behind her back and an apple was held tight in place to gag her screams.

"Hagar, get the new girl into the cage and chain her down." The little man was in a rage and he pulled free a little bull whip from inside his coat. "And you girls get to your tent immediately. We'll have no more nonsense from you tonight."

With a crack of the little whip the girls were sent scurrying off, screaming and giggling as they went.

"Those girls will be the death of me."

The strong man opened part of the cage and threw the girl in. He followed her and pulled another chain from under the dirty straw. He attached it to her wrists with a heavy padlock. He then double checked to see if it was secure with a good solid yank. The whole cage moved but the chain remained bolted to the floor. "She's secure, Mr Thumtumbulous. She's not going anywhere tonight."

"Good, but to make sure, Ingrid, give these lovely people something to help them sleep.

The bearded lady took out a medical bag from under her gypsy garb and removed a hypodermic and a small glass vile of pink liquid. She took a fat hit from the bottle and entered the cage. She plunged the needle into the neck of the woman and filled her with half of the pink fluid.

Just the idea of another needle entering his body in such a way made Chris lightheaded and he slumped rearward. The chains held his limp body at a strange angle, with his feet planted firmly in the dung on the floor.

"I guess he won't need any, Boss?" asked the deep, baritone voice of the hairy woman with the needle.

"Give him a shot anyway just to be on the safe side. Send the Fun Girls out for another woman. I don't want to take any more chances."

It was the last thing he heard as he blacked out. A sliver of ruptured yellow rubber with a knot in it hung forlornly from the eye of his penis.

TEN

IN THE DARK THE WET STONE STEPS WERE MORE than arduous. The wind wasn't helping matters either as it sent the rain in like pellets. Droplets bounced off of the hard stone over their head making the group wetter as they made their assent.

At the top they found themselves on a vast field with what looked like a huge oblong box of black granite in the distance.

The white faced clown pointed. "That's where we are headed. That's the Lonely Fortress."

"That's got to be a mile away." Ruby was less than impressed.

"A mile and a half as the crow flies," the clown beamed back.

Gregor

"I'll be fucking dead by the time we get there." Pickles was feeling worse for wear but the tranquilisers were doing their job. He'd almost forgotten that he was soaked to the skin.

"Come on, the longer we hang around the wetter we're going to get." Capo was off, almost skipping down a gravel track towards the ominous black box.

Ruby shouted after him: "I can't get wetter than this, you arsehole." Even her jacket pockets were full of water.

"It's okay," Capo called back. "There'll be a change of clothes waiting when we get there. Maybe even a cup of tea, too."

"I fucking hate that guy already." Ruby turned to see Pickles bending over furiously dry heaving. "We need to get you somewhere warm and get you something to eat."

She pulled the soaked clown upright and started to drag him the mile and a half to the Lonely Fortress. Pickles staggered and groaned all the way there. The tranquilizers had taken more of a hold than he'd first figured. Maybe he shouldn't have had six of them and only two like the bottle stated.

The weather didn't let up for a moment and only seemed to get heavier the closer they got the black shape on the horizon. When the finally got to anything that looked like a gate, the walls of the Fortress loomed high over them.

"If you'll follow me, we'll find some towels for you." Capo rang a bell over the gate and a door in the wall opened. A huge white face clown stepped out in heavy riot armour. He slipped a ring of keys off of his belt and fumbled at the gate.

"Capo, I take it he's the one taking *you-know-who* off the island."

"Shush!" Capo waved a finger in front of his mouth. "It's meant to be a surprise."

Pickles was far too high to register what they were saying, but Ruby heard. "Take who off the island?" She asked.

"Go through to the holding area. You can get changed. There's refreshments and fresh make-up, as well." The guard ushered the group through the door.

"Take who off the fucking island?" Ruby insisted but she was pushed through a second door into a brightly lit canteen. It was lined with folding tables and plastic chairs. On one of the tables was a pile of towels, a make-up box and lime green overalls. A microwave and a stack of ready meals sat next to various coloured bottles of fizzy pop and tubs of ice cream.

"You two get changed. You'll have to wait a few hours in this area until the rest of the council are here." Capo made his way out of the room. "So try and get some rest." He closed the door behind him and locked it.

"TAKE WHO OFF THE FUCKING ISLAND?!" Ruby stamped her foot in a tantrum but her protesting fell on deaf ears.

Pickles was already laying down on one of the tables. He was as good as passed out so Ruby set about stripping him and towelling him dry before sorting herself out.

"You can dress your own damn self," She told him, flopping the overalls over the naked clown on the table. She wrapped his damp towel and stuffed it under his lolloping head and he began to snore loudly. He was done for a while.

"Stick a fucking fork in him."

Ruby towel herself down and slipped into the green overalls. Then she set about applying her make-up from the well-stocked kit. Her wig was ruined so she had to make do with tying her shoulder length black hair up in a pineapple on the top of her head.

Then she checked out the food. Microwave sausage and mash, toad in the hole with gravy, roast chicken dinner, macaroni and cheese with bacon, cottage pie. She chose the mac and cheese and opened a tub of cookie dough ice cream while she waited for her meal to ping.

Gregor

The meal exploded in the microwave well before the allotted five minutes were up. Ruby was always disappointed when food burst before the ping.

It was a mess in there but Ruby scraped what was edible back into its container and took her food over to an adjacent table to where Pickles was sleeping. His hand twitched like a dog having a running dream and he made mumbled noises mixed in with deep grunts and exhalations.

"Sawing logs," Ruby muttered as she shovelled a spoonful of the gooey pasta into her mouth only to find its temperature was that of lava. "FUCKING... PRICKS... CUNT... FUCK!" She followed the burning mouthful with a helping of the cookie dough. "Fuck that's hot," she exclaimed through a wad of molten cheese and dribbling ice cream.

It was then that she noticed the security camera in the far corner. A little red light blinked under the lens. It was recording.

"What the fuck are you looking at?" Ruby showed her distain at the invasion of privacy by flipping the camera off. She grabbed a handful of her left tit and poking out her tongue then returned to her food. She had forgotten how hot the first spoonful was and was soon panicking for the ice cream again.

"FUCK... SHIT... BOLLOCKS... FUCK!"

After eating Ruby wrapped a towel over her shoulders and climbed up onto the table. She too needed some rest. Ruby pulled the towel over her head to cut out the light from the fluorescent strip bulbs above them. The roof of her mouth was still tingling from the stupidly hot food. It had formed a blister and she drifted off to sleep while tonguing it.

Ruby didn't know she was asleep until she was awoken by a strange sound. It was like a gargling noise and it was right by her head. She opened her eyes to see Pickles standing over her naked with freshly applied face paint chugging a two litre bottle of strawberry fizzy pop.

He drained the whole bottle, threw the crushed plastic bottle to the ground then released the biggest belch Ruby had ever heard. It made Pickles' flaccid penis quiver from his gullet vibrations.

"I feel so much better," he said, taking a wide stance and putting his hands on his hips. His cock was now only inches away from Ruby's face. "Now, what's for eats in this fucking shithole?"

ELEVEN

DEEP UNDERGROUND A RHYTHMICAL POUNDING resonated through the earth.

Pools of collected water in the subterranean corridors rippled with vibration with every booming thud. It was almost mechanical, low, the sort of sound that hit you in the gut and made your bladder twitch.

A door frame rattled, the windows shuddered and a mug of coffee in the security booth was slowly making its way to the edge of the table.

One of the two security guards in clown make-up on duty saw it teetering and placed it in the safety of the centre of the table.

"He's sure pissed off tonight. Should we gas him again?"

"Nah, the doctor said we can only gas him twice a night. They don't want to fuck up his nervous system or something."

"That thing has a nervous system?" The guard took a swig from the vibrating cup. "You don't think he can get out of there do you?"

"Dunno, but he got out on floor two this one time."

"Bullshit!"

"He straight up tore the cell door clean off. Then the crazy fuck ripped up some nurse like she was a bread roll." The guard took a little joint from his top pocket and lit it. "It took all night to get the fucker down, even after they filled him with enough tranquiliser to put the world asleep."

"Bull fucking shit!"

"Nah, my buddy was there, saw the whole thing. He said they just kept shooting him and shooting him. In the end they had to run him over with the doctor's car." He puffed at the joint then passed it to his counterpart. "Then they stood round him in a big circle jerk and just kept shooting him with tranq-dart until he was out. It took about five guys with ten darts each."

"No way, the fucker would be dead! Any fucker would be dead." The joint smoke bit the back of the guard's throat causing him to splutter as he exhaled. He passed it back. "Smooth."

"That's why he's down here. (Puff puff) They reckon he can't get out from here on account of the walls being too thick and those doors can withstand a missile attack. That room used to be some Fort Knox type safe or something."

The first guard peered at the security monitors. In the darkness he could see the thing moving around. Every now and then the prisoner would take a swing with a sledge hammer sized fist at the ground. Each punch sent a deep thud vibrating through the ground.

"He's really going to town on the floor tonight. Are you sure he can't get out?"

"Yeah, we'll be fine." The second guard took one last pull on the joint before putting it out under his boot. "The storm always sets them off. Count yourself lucky you're not on one of the busier floors. This guy's a piece of piss compared to the bigger wards."

"Yeah, but I'm just worried that door won't hold out. He's dead angry tonight."

"Sitting in here watching that fucker beat the floor up is better than trying to contain thirty psychos throwing their shit at you, believe me."

"Yeah I guess."

The thuds from the cell stopped and both guards leaned in to the screens to see if he had passed out. The screen looked almost completely black. Even with the little light let in by the four inch thick toughened glass the cell looked empty.

"I don't like this. I can't see a fucking thing on this monitor."

"So get down there and check on him."

"You can suck my balls."

"Don't be such a pussy. Hell, he's probably just asleep. The motherfucker got himself worn out from all that punching."

"Well, I ain't going down there. You can fuck that shit."

"I'm telling you he can't get out."

"What if he's already out?"

"What, you think he punched all the way outta that cell?" Guard two folded his arms. "It's got a floor made of ten feet of reinforced concrete! You think he just punched his way through it?"

The two men stared at each other for a moment then grabbed their batons and riot helmets and left the booth with a little jog in their step.

They both hit the wall at the same time, one guard on each side of the huge vault like door.

"Take a look." Guard number one signalled to his colleague.

"Fuck you, you take a look." Guard one returned the comment with the finger.

"I made the tea and brought the weed so it's your turn."

"How fucking old are you?"

"Blow me, it's your turn, you look."

Gregor

Reluctantly he started to peer into the glass and reached for the light switch. "I still think we should have gassed him."

The light almost blinded him as its stark brightness suddenly hit his eyes but almost straight away he saw the man monster standing at the back of the cell. He was a mass of pumped up seven foot muscle. His fists were all bloody and strapped with bits of his ripped up green overall. His mop of thick dark hair dripped sweat down his smeared mime artist style makeup.

Bloody patches on the floor marked each spot he'd punched. It looked like a one colour twister mat.

Then, without the faintest sign, he rushed at the door stopping dead an inch away from the glass. The security guard on the other side fell back followed by a huge thud from a punch against the door. The guard could see the dead eyes of the monster on the other side looking down at him.

Then they pulled away and the floor punching started again.

Guard number two burst out laughing, "Holy shit! You might want to check your pants."

"You fucking knew that would happen."

"Of course," he continued to chuckle and started back down the corridor to the booth, "Johnny does that shit all the time. Speaking of shit, you might want to hit the bathroom. I think baby went boom-boom."

"Fuck you and fuck that giant asshole, hope he rots!" Guard number one got to his feet and stormed towards the security booth passing his buddy in huge determined strides. "I'm gassing the prick."

TWELVE

PICKLES WAS SLAMMING TOAD IN THE HOLE IN HIS FACE like a man that had never seen real food before. Spots of gravy dotted his mirrored aviators as he thrashed away at the ready meal with his plastic knife and fork. He had already eaten a tub of ice cream and a tray of cottage pie and didn't look like he was stopping after this round.

The floor was littered with empty pop bottles and ready meal wrappers.

"You," Ruby looked away in disgust, "… are a fucking animal."

"Shut up, woman." A morsel of sausage hung from the corner of his mouth like a cigar as he chewed. "This is the first meal I've had in over a week, I need my strength."

His comedown was nothing but a pale memory and a slight headache like a nightmare he'd had but could barely remember. He was finding it hard to remember anything.

"And we were on a boat?" He scratched his ear with the fork.

"Yes, we were on a fucking boat."

"Hah, I had forgotten about that." He stuffed another sausage in his mouth.

"But you brought us here. You knew the route we took; you knew we had to take a boat." Ruby was flabbergasted.

"Yeah, but I get these dead spots in my memory sometimes when I'm rattling." He chugged at another bottle of pop, belched then continued, "And that was a bad one. I actually thought I was going to die." He laughed to himself as he finished the last bite. "Any chance you can put that other toad in the hole on for us?"

Ruby got up in a huff. "What did your last slave die of?"

"Not doing as they were fucking told." He finished the bottle of pop. "And get me some more drink. I wish this was beer."

The door they came in opened and both of them turned to see Capo entering. He was still smiling past his sad make-up.

"You two look suitably refreshed, good." He came into the canteen and sat down with the pair. "You'll be meeting with the council soon. They're all on the island and getting ready."

"But is there anymore toad in the hole?" Pickles looked over the top of his shades. It was the first time in days his eyes weren't bloodshot.

"Mr Pickles, there will be plenty of time for eating after the meeting." Capo waved an arm towards the door.

"Let's just get it over with." Ruby was up and leaving.

"But I'm still hungry." He shook his head and reluctantly got up from the canteen table. "This isn't right. The second I get my appetite back and I have to leave all the food."

Pickles stuffed a tub of bubble gum sprinkles ice cream into his rucksack and followed. He was always hungry after a long session. Probably down to the fact he wouldn't eat for a week. He always felt so alive after a binge but he knew he'd be back in that dark hole soon enough.

They made their collective way through another set of doors then another and another until they found themselves in a long corridor made from the same black granite as the outside walls. Along the corridor were white doors, each with a viewing window in the centre with a number painted in black.

"These are the cells where the patients are kept." Capo was still smiling though it seemed a little crocked, not his usual demeanour in the halls of the great insane. "We have many celebrities here."

Under the windows hung cards with the details of each of the room's inhabitants. Pickles took up on of the cards for room three.

"Gary the Musical Clown. Holy shit, I've heard of him."

"Few haven't, Mr Pickles." Capo edged over to the door where Pickles was standing. "He was a great children's entertainer but he had a dark secret and by the end it consumed him."

"Yeah, they found all those dead orphans buried in his garden. He was growing potatoes over them or something."

"Cabbages, in fact. Over there in room six is Gum Shoes the clown. A very sad case, indeed."

Ruby bounded over to the viewing window just in time to see a sad faced hobo clown stuff his hand up his own arsehole.

"Oh my god, that's fucking disgusting." Ruby held her hand to her mouth as the clown in room six pulled a fistful of his own faecal matter out and started to eat it.

"Yes, he got slightly carried away in a traveling act. Instead of throwing buckets of glitter over the crowd he started using his own waste." Capo shook his head. "It was all quite a mess. Then there's Sandro Salini in room nine, the fine Auguste clown. He was caught during a home invasion."

"Didn't he eat some of the people he killed?" Pickles asked as he peered into number nine to see a room painted with the number 17 over and over in various coloured crayon all over the walls.

"That's right Mr Pickles; he killed seventeen families coast to coast traveling with a big top show. A family in every state he visited. While the rest of the troop slept he was out enjoying himself."

They continued down the corridor towards an elevator.

"Have you ever heard of the Flying Malvinas'?" Capo stopped and pointed at door twenty one. "Well, we have the one that's still alive. After a trapezes accident that left the Marco Malvinas paralyzed the younger brother Beppo went mad with grief and performed experiments on his prone brother to try and get him to walk again."

Gregor

"That's just bizarre." Ruby looked in through the viewing window to see a white face clown rolling around on the floor strapped up tight in a strait jacket.

"It's said that when they found the pair Beppo was wearing his still alive brother as a kind of suit and was attempting to cartwheel around the centre ring of their circus. Needless to say he resides with us now, for his own good of course."

"So, what about Johnny Palladuchi?" Ruby wanted to join in the 'name the fucked up clown' game with the boys. Capo almost froze to the spot with the mere mention of the name and carried on towards the elevator. "Johnny Palladuchi, he's in here, right?" Ruby was determined to get an answer from the now panicked Capo.

"Erm, Ms Ruby, we tend not to say his name that often around here."

"Why not? Will he appear if you say his fucking name three times or something?"

"Yes. Something like that. Now if you'll follow me we'll continue to the top floor and the conference room. They'll be waiting."

The steel doors slid open with the touch of a big red button that read 'push'. They collectively stepped into the waiting lift. The doors slid closed with a 'ping' and Ruby immediately thought of the microwave. She hoped she wouldn't burst before it went ping again.

From a tiny speaker in the corner a Bontempi organ version of Wham's 'Club Tropicana' was being piped into the ascending metal box containing the clowns. Pickles couldn't help but tap his foot to the cheesy tune. Ruby elbowed his ribs and glared at him. "What?" He shrugged and continued his micro-bop to the pop classic hammed up further by the cheap sound of the Bontempi.

Ruby crossed her arms. "I fucking hate this tune."

THIRTEEN

SHARON WAS TAKING THE SHOPPING OUT TO THE CAR IN the trolley. She would often do the shopping late night, less people around to bump trollies with. Shop zombies her husband called them.

Sharon was inclined to agree with him.

There was something about a supermarket. When the majority of people enter it that their IQ dramatically drops. People become rude, selfish and ultimately stupid in a shopping centre. And when they have their children with them, forget about it, lumbering cattle with children running under their feet.

This is why Sharon was here at eleven at night. The day her local supermarket went 24hour was one of unmentionable joy.

No more getting barged by overweight morons. No more screaming kids throwing tantrums. No more queuing at the checkouts and having to wait an extra ten minutes because the people in front would suddenly remember that they forgot to get milk the second the checkout girl started putting their groceries through.

Why were people so fucking stupid?

No, now it was just her. She could take her sweet time around the store with next to no one in it, then out and home. She would be home with her feet up watching Ghost Adventures in a matter of minutes.

That was another advantage, no traffic.

She chuckled to herself as she loaded the back of her car with the groceries, shut the boot and made her way back to return the trolley across the deserted car park.

It was when she took her pound out that she heard a whistle coming from the multi-story car park. Not a wolf whistle, more a melody, a 'look this way' sort of tune. She looked up to the top floor to see a flash of green hair duck down behind the wall.

Fucking kids playing, the silly buggers.

Gregor

She shrugged it off. She knew that skaters would sometimes plot up there and do whatever teenage kids did on the roofs of multi-story car parks.

Drugs probably.

Sharon hurried back to her car followed by another whistle, this time from some bushes over by the bottle bank. Something tipped over a box of jam jars by the recycling bins and Sharon snapped her head around to see who was there.

Another flash of colour, this time red hair. It darted off into the bushes.

"Look, who's there?" Sharon fumbled with her car keys. "This isn't funny you know."

There was another whistle, this time from behind a delivery van. It was accompanied by a flash of pink hair. Sharon got the key in the door and scrambled into the car. She slammed the door behind her and hit the central locking. She whipped on her seat belt and started the car.

Something moved on the back seat and she looked into the rear view mirror only to find herself eye to eye with a girl in clown make-up staring back at her.

Before she had time to scream a chemical soaked sponge was shoved over her face as the girl in the back seat leached forward and wrapped her arm around her neck and the head rest. The chemical worked quickly and Sharon could feel herself start to float away and her eyes rolled into her head.

That was when the clown girl put the bag over her head and the stink of the chemical finally overpowered her. It sent Sharon flying out of her body into a rich orange sky, high over the town and away into the blackness of space.

Motion and flashes of light accompanied with voices and music. From the shade of the hessian bag she could see shadows moving around her. She was coming round but her body felt fuzzy. Her mind was in and out of the dream space the chemical had placed her. Every now and then another whiff would send her crashing back into the darkness until the sounds; lights and movement would bring her momentarily back into reality.

There was a fire in the back of her nose from the liquid used to knock her out. It felt like someone had poured boiling sand into her nostrils. The bag on her head stank of it, that pear drop smell of alcohol and acetone, sweet, viscous.

A bump in the road woke her fully from her drugged slumber as her body was flung across the floor of the van.

All around her the sounds of girls having sex with each other and a man's voice, deep and Scandinavian sounding called back from the driving seat: "You girls might want to get it together, we're nearly home."

Home.

The word bounced around inside Sharon's aching head like a ping pong ball and she started to cry when the realisation of her situation kicked in. Would she ever see her home again?

Her kids. Her boyfriend, even that horrid cat that hated her. The warmth and cosiness of her bed, the power-shower they had fitted after their holiday to Majorca.

The van came to an abrupt halt and Sharon slid back down towards the driver. She heard the back doors open and the girls around her got out then someone grabbed her by the ankles and pulled her from the van. She landed hard on her back, knocking the wind out of her.

It was raining, the bag over her head instantly soaked through from the heavy storm and she was manhandled to her feet and dragged across the wet ground.

The bag was ripped off her head to reveal that she was being dragged by a muscle bound man in a leopard print thong and a

Gregor

woman with a huge beard. They were surrounded by naked girls with clown faces and brightly coloured hair.

A huge wave of water hit her full in the face as she was dragged through the flap of a big top circus tent. Animals paced in cages; tigers, an elephant, bears, chimpanzees all looking at her. They whooped and growled and hissed at the arrival of the new attraction.

Sharon wanted to scream her lungs out but her brain just couldn't allow it. She was in shock at what was happening. They stopped at a cage covered in a red and white canvas and the strong man opened the gate.

The bearded lady shoved her in and she fell into a pile of dank straw that reeked of piss and amimal shit and the strongman locked the gate behind her.

It took a moment as she squinted in the dull light of the cage then let out an almighty scream as she was faced with an unconscious man hanging by his wrists from the ceiling and a woman chained to the floor.

"Stop screaming, we don't want the little man to come back," the chained woman whispered.

FOURTEEN

THE EXECUTIVE CONFERENCE ROOM WAS PLUSH.

Deepest crimson curtains and rich mahogany shelving with a vast conference table made from a single slice of Canadian redwood was circled with high backed leather chairs. At the far end was a book case the length of the wall filled with expensive looking collections of leather bound books. Its centrepiece was a painting of a sinister looking clown handing a little girl a red balloon.

"These pricks have got some money." Pickles flopped down into one of the chairs and threw his bag onto the endangered conference table.

"Yeah, was this the place you came to last time?" Ruby sat down in an opposite chair.

"Nah, last time it was in this high-rise skyscraper thing in the city, some sort of bank building."

Capo was looking more than nervous. "Well, if you'll excuse me, I have to be getting back to my duties." He bowed and hurried for the elevator.

"Don't be a stranger," Pickles called out behind him as the lift doors shut with a ping. "Glad that fuckers gone, never liked people that are too happy."

"Speaking of happy, you've perked up a bit. You were on deaths door." Ruby put her elbows on the table and cradled her head in her hands.

"Yeah, amazing what a few hours' sleep and some food can do for one's constitution. That reminds me." He grabbed up the rucksack and dived in for the tub of ice-cream. He beamed when his hand gripped around the wax paper tub. Its sides made his hands reassuringly cold and wet. "Ah, mother's milk."

He ate greedily using his fingers as a spoon, dribbling down his chin. It was at this moment that the council entered the room. Pickles froze with his fingers in his mouth and a bubble of goo popped in the corner of his mouth.

The five men strode in wrapped in black cloaks, each in make-up representing the five houses of clownery.

There was Patches Theobald, the councillor that had sent Pickles the summons representing the white face clowns, Gallochini representing the Auguste clowns, Denzo representing the hobos. Jean-Pierre Franco represented the mimes and Hacksaw McGraw representing the Rodeo clowns.

Each man in a fine tailored suit underneath their black robes. They in turn bowed to each other and took up seats across from the Ruby and Pickles.

Gregor

Patches Theobald sat in the middle and took out a stack of papers from a red briefcase and shuffled them on the table. Without saying one word he threw a file over to Pickles and sat back down linking his fingers in front of his lips.

The council sat completely silent staring straight at Pickles.

A dollop of ice cream fell off Pickles' chin into his lap as he stared back over his mirrored aviators. "What?"

"If you would open the file, Pickles, we can continue." Theobald was stern and sounded like he had smoked too many cigarettes with an air of contempt in his voice towards the junky clown.

"Oh, right you are." He sucked the last of the bubble gum sprinkles from his fingers and reached for the folder flipping it open and removing the papers inside.

"In this dossier you will find the details of a one Ringmaster Thumtumbulous, he has become a menace to the council and has set up an unsanctioned circus outside the small town of Breen, it would seem he's assembled a militia of freaks and clowns." Theobald shifted in his chair. "He has been putting on... unsavoury performances."

"Unsavoury?" Pickles studied a blown up photograph of a dwarf in a top hat secretly snapped as he took a leak into some bushes. "What sort of unsavoury?"

"Let's just say the population of Breen, albeit small, has lost numbers dramatically." Theobald leaned in. "And it's not just Breen that's losing people. Many of the towns along the coast have reports of missing persons, taken from their homes or while out at night. We are finding it more than a little embarrassing."

"Not as little as this prick." Pickles turned the photo and held it for the council to see and gave it a wave. "Look at his little dick." He beamed.

Theobald's fist slammed down on the conference table. "This is no laughing matter!" The room was ringing with his tone of voice. "We have spent a great deal of time surveying what we, the council, are able to do on this."

"And you want me to go in there undercover and take this midget spit-fuck out, right?"

"By no means, Mr Pickles. We want you to attend one of their performances posing as an audience member."

"So this is information gathering?" Ruby chipped in.

"Silence, bitch!" Hacksaw McGraw bellowed at Ruby, shrinking her into her chair. "You are only allowed here because this fuck-stick can't function on his own. You're only here to make sure he doesn't overdose on the job and let the hit man escape." McGraw realised he had said a little too much as Theobald and the other council clowns glared at him.

"Hit man, what do you mean hit man? What's going down here?" Pickles threw the folder back on to the table.

"Thank you, Mr McGraw." Theobald straightened his tie. "Mr Pickles, the other part of the operation is to take our chosen enforcer to the underground carnival to eliminate this threat and then return him safely to us."

"Wait – you want me to do what now?" Pickles threw himself back into his chair and rubbed at his temples. "I'm not a fucking baby sitter."

"We have chosen you because you have the right skill set that we need; a certain level of debasement and low moral ethics that make you the right man not to mention you will be generously rewarded." Theobald returned his hand to the praying position in front of his mouth. His big red nose touched the tips of his fingers.

With the words 'rewarded' and 'generously' he almost forgot Theobald had also said 'low moral ethics' and Pickles' interest twitched. He knew the council was loaded and it could be just the

Gregor

break he needed to get as far away from this life as he could. Maybe by that beach hut in Honolulu he had always dreamed of.

"Okay, say I agree, who will I be transporting?"

"Like I say the council are prepared to offer you a quite handsome amount…"

"Who will I be transporting?"

"The mass murderer; Johnny Palladuchi."

It was almost like a bomb had gone off and suddenly been paused in time. Nothing moved, not even particles of oxygen.

Pickles stood up and beckoned Ruby to do the same. "Well it's been nice catching up. Come on Ruby, we are leaving."

"Mr Pickles." Theobald bellowed.

"No, no, please I'm sure you are busy people. Let's just call this a miss hit and we can all get on with our lives. Come on Ruby."

"Mr Pickles, if you refuse we will have no alternative but to detain you and your companion as patients within the prison, general circulation, maximum security. You will never leave this place alive."

On the one hand Pickles was facing life imprisonment with some of the worst monsters the human race ever coughed out of its anus, on the other hand he was to take one of the most dangerous men alive to the circus.

He paused and mulled it over for a moment. "Tell me again about this generous reward."

FIFTEEN

"THAT'S IT; NOW SPREAD YOUR ARSEHOLE, BABY."

Gibbon was up close with his video camera as a girl in an American Indian headdress gaped her caved-in butthole. Behind him was the guy dressed as General Custer that had just pulled his dick free from the naughty native girl's sphincter.

"You want me back in?" The guy said messing with his stick-on moustache.

"Yeah, give me a moment then it's from behind then we'll move into missionary for the pop shot, right on the belly." Gibbon playfully smacked the girls arse and came around to start recording the Generals re-entry. "You're doing good guys, this is better than the last few I've done."

He shuddered when he thought of the crack head blowjob-for-drugs scene he had already shot that morning and the beating the poor girl had taken when she spat instead of swallowed.

Thank fuck this was just a vanilla shoot.

Later on he'd have to shoot a tramp gangbang. He was not so happy with that thought. He hated the way the tramps would stink up the place and try and steal everything that wasn't nailed down. He knew now why so many skin heads set fire to them in the park.

Gibbon clipped the camera into a waiting tripod just as his phone started to ring in his pocket. He pulled it out to see the name flashing on the screen.

It was Pickles.

"Shit, hang on guys, I have to take this." He made for the container door. "Just keep it hard, suck him off for a while, you know."

The rain from the night before had cleared but it had given everything a damp smell and it was worse out in the yard of the container park. Gibbon held the phone to his head as he squelched across the soft ground.

"Word up?"

"Gibbon, am I glad you picked up." Pickles sounded worried.

"What's wrong, is it Ruby?"

"Ruby's fine. I need a favour, a big one."

Gibbon didn't like the sound of that. "What kind of favour?"

"I need you to fill the boot of your shit box motor with as many weapons as you can get your hands on and bring them to the town of Breen."

"Weapons?"

"Guns, knives, bats, swords, petrol bombs, fuck it, egg whisks. Whatever the hell you can get your fucking hands on, brother."

"Then you want me to drive to Breen. You know there's a storm coming tonight, right?"

"Not tonight, now, as soon as possible. I'm not fucking around on this one." There was a pause of static. "I'll give you ten grand if you can get here in the next four fucking hours."

"Ten grand?" Gibbon wanted to be sure he heard correctly.

"Ten fucking grand," Pickles repeated like a foul mouthed parrot.

"I can be on the road in twenty minutes."

Gibbon hung up and rushed back inside the container. General Custer looked a little flustered when Gibbon burst through the door.

"I'm sorry, man, I couldn't help it, it was too good, I couldn't hold on. If you give me like fifteen minutes I can go again."

Gibbon looked at the Indian girl wiping the spunk from her chin. "Fuck that shit, you can stay here and shoot your own movie or fuck the fuck off but I have to go." He whipped a blanket off of a beat up footlocker next to the bed and fumbled with the combination lock.

"Say, what's in the box?" The guy couldn't have sounded more like a dumb arse if he had tried.

"Guns." Gibbon flipped open the lid and pulled out two huge assault rifles. "Big fuck off guns, ya fucking dunce."

With the car loaded up Gibbon was ready to hit the road.

Along with the assault rifles there was a sawn off shotgun, three pistols including the revolver in his glove box, a hand grenade, three sticks of dynamite and a set of brass knuckles. And with a little gentle threatening the General Custer guy had given up his baseball bat from his own car.

The girl in the headdress could only find a set of hair straighteners in her car. Gibbon politely declined the offer.

"So you two are gonna stay and finish the shoot and film the tramp gang bang?"

"It's the least we can do to help out." The General fiddled with his moustache again. "Besides, I've shot loads of POV stuff. I know how to work a camera."

"Cool beans. Just be sure and lock up after and don't let those dirty vagrants don't steal any of the gear."

Gibbon didn't want to stay and trade anymore banter with the dumb naked John standing in the yard with his dick swinging in the breeze and slammed shut the door to his car. He was contemplating putting the gun back in his mouth for a moment but then thought of the ten grand. That would keep him going for a good six months.

The car rattled to life and he pulled out of the yard onto the streets of Cheapside. It was a good three hour drive to Breen but with a selection of snacks, energy drinks and the radio he might just be able to stand it.

The radio honked out some bubble gum crap as he made for the motorway. He would have to stop at some services and get a couple of rat burgers and one of those huge drinks that make you want to piss directly after finishing the last drop.

He thought of what he would do with the ten grand.

Maybe get away, start again, something new, totally different from the cycle of shit that he was revolving around in at the moment. He knew only too well that he was on the verge of

Gregor

snapping, losing his shit and taking out the next 'all dude junkie gangbang'. That's why he kept the guns in the container.

That's why every now and then he'd sit in his car with a gun in his mouth.

Ten grand! This could be the fresh start he was looking for. Gibbon turned up the trash radio and for the first time in a long time he smiled.

SIXTEEN

"HE'S COMING." **PICKLES CANCELED THE CALL BUTTON** on his phone and turned to Ruby. "Say's he'll meet us outside of Breen in a few hours. It sounds like he's got a few toys for us too."

"I don't like all this you know." Ruby was sat cross-legged on the floor of the corridor that led to the maximum security cells. "Not one bit, no sir."

"You think I do? Do you really think I want to be anywhere near this place, anywhere near that fucking psycho Palladuchi?" He was into another tub of the complimentary ice cream and on the verge of brain freeze. "That Patches Theobald has given me no choice. We have to. I don't want to spend any more time in this place let alone end up being one of the doped up inmates throwing my shit up the walls."

"You'd be in your element in here." She honked a little bike horn she had stolen from the conference room at Pickles twice. "Free drugs, all the ice cream you can eat, interesting conversation."

"Interesting conversation? Have you ever talked to one of these fuck ups?"

"I was talking to you on the way here wasn't I?"

"Fuck you."

"Well you have been rather away with the fairies."

"I mean one of these proper nutters, one of the window lickers?" Pickles was tempted to dump the tub over her head. "I worked with this guy called Bumpy the Juggler many moons ago for about a year. His wife had left him and he had a bit of a break down. Thought the police had put cameras and recording equipment in the cracks in the walls."

"What?" Ruby sounded intrigued.

"Yeah, straight up. When you talked to him it was like he's a normal guy but the shit he came out with was completely out there. I mean it was all conspiracy theories and aliens and shit." Pickles wiped his nose with the sleeve of the green boiler suit. "Prick killed himself in the end. He hung himself off a bridge and a truck hit him."

"Get the fuck out of here." Ruby shook her head.

"No lie, apparently he swung back up onto the bridge like a conker on a bootlace."

"Now I know you're fucking lying."

"I'm not. It was in the papers and everything."

Ruby almost managed a smile as the security doors at the end of the corridor opened slowly with a 'CLUNK'. The sound caused a ball to swell in her throat and Pickles turned away.

"When this fucker comes out try not to make eye contact with him." Pickles hands trembled slightly. "I've heard he doesn't like it when he gets stared down."

The security door slowly swung open scrapping the floor. It was accompanied by a blast of cool air into the corridor. The silhouette of three men cut through the gloom of the maximum security unit.

One shadow was gigantic.

"Holy fuck sticks." Ruby shook her head at the size of the man being escorted out by a heavily armoured security guard and Patches Theobald. "That is one big fucking bastard."

"Shut the fuck up, Roobs!" Pickles whispered sternly. "Let's try not to piss him off before we've even got out of here."

"I know that but look at the size of the fucker," Ruby whispered back. She was trying her best not to stare and failing miserably.

Behind the guard and Theobald was a man mountain. The mass of thick muscle lumbered. His ankles were chained together and a huge metal box was bolted around his hands. His arms were strapped to his body restricting his movement further.

Thick black hair hung over his dark eyes. His face was painted pure white with only a single blood red tear under his left eye.

Ruby shuddered to look at the beast and it seemed like a shadow followed him as the hulk made his way down the corridor. She could almost swear that the temperature had dropped and for a moment she thought she heard a church bell tolling the coming of a distant funeral procession.

Without Ruby's knowledge, Pickles had edged behind her. If Palladuchi was going to riot now he could at least use her as a human shield when the punching started.

Theobald gestured to the guard and the party stopped halfway down the corridor. He continued to where Pickles was cowering behind Ruby who just couldn't stop staring.

"You will sign this contract." The clown councillor took out a digital tablet and handed it to Pickles over Ruby's shoulder. "This is to signify that you now have custody of the prisoner for forty-eight hours. You will take him to Breen; infiltrate the illegal carnival to take as many recognisance notes as you can then send the prisoner to eliminate any and all hostiles therein. When this is done you will return with the prisoner where payment will be sent to your account."

"What's stopping him from ripping us apart and escaping the second he gets to the mainland?" Pickles was concerned.

"You will notice the collar around the prisoner's neck." Theobald held up a little remote control. "This device has two settings. One is a shocker. If the prisoner becomes restless a quick jolt from this will calm him down. The second is an explosive. If he becomes out of control, well, you get the idea."

Ruby took the remote. "Give him a buzz if he gets agitated. If he goes mad blow the pricks head off."

Palladuchi grunted and tilted his head. He wasn't fond of being called a prick, even by a girl. He started to wonder what her blood would look like on his fists and smiled at her.

Ruby shuddered at the crack of a grin that appeared in the monster-man's white make-up and averted her gaze towards the floor.

"So let me get this right," Pickles held out the remote, "If this guy gets out of hand you want me to blow his head off with this thing?"

"That is correct Mr Pickles. He understands the concept and will be on his best behaviour." Theobald turned to the lump of psychopathic killing machine. "You understand, don't you Johnny?"

The giants head snapped towards the councillor and he smiled again holding his hands up in prayer and nodding in an over acted mime that would freeze the blood of Satan himself.

"Yes, the sooner you get under way the better. I'll leave Bubbles here as part of the escort." He motioned towards the armoured guard who dry gulped what little air he could. "I'll see you on the other side."

Patches Theobald marched on leaving the obviously petrified guard and the maniac in the capable hands of Pickles and his female ward. All three looked up at the monstrous grinning mime and trembled. The giant looked back.

Gregor

"So what do we do now?" Ruby said still in awe of the beast in front of her. Something tingled in her pussy and she could only figure it was terror.

The guard piped up with an edge of nerves in his voice, "We get to the dock and take the boat up the coast to Breen. I report back and then we get our next set of orders."

"Then it all kicks off, right?" Pickles enquired.

"I guess so," the guard returned.

"And do you swear that you're going to be on your best behaviour until we let you off the chain, Johnny?" Pickles felt a dry ball stop the words from being pronounced properly and turned his voice into a squeak.

Palladuchi held his boxed hands up again and crossed his heart as he nodded. This time he wasn't smiling. This time he looked more than serious.

SEVENTEEN

HAGAR WAS AT THE WHEEL OF THE 'FUN BUS', a brightly painted van that could have passed for a hippy wagon if it wasn't for the 'Circus Outlandish' logo painted decoratively down both sides.

The windows of the vehicle were tinted in a deep black and the wheels were twenty inch aftermarket six spokes on fat tires. The exhaust was the width of a baked bean tin and it honked out a deep engine rumble that sounded like thunder and mechanical flatulence. It coughed fire with each gear change as the van sped through the night.

His passenger was the bearded lady who had stripped off her gypsy rag and was now in a tight yellow bikini. Her big hairy tits wobbled from the vibration of the van and she played slowly with her pussy. Her hands stuffed down the front of the yellow thong so crammed with pubic hair it looked like her vagina had trapped Sly Stone and only the top of his head had escaped the cunt's clutches.

In the back a pack of junkies were bound and gagged with duct tape. Hagar hand his hirsute girlfriend had been into the town to scoop up some vagabonds to staff the fair, the attractions without targets. Breen had lost some more of its degenerate inhabitants tonight but this scum would not be missed. Just another group of down and outs that's they had rounded up in one of the old shut down fishery buildings.

The throw a dart stall, the pitch and dunk, the whack a mole, all of the stalls needed fodder to make the crowds go crazy.

Even the hog roast wagon would need a couple to keep the masses happy; nothing like a well cooked, spit roasted tramp with a dollop of apple sauce in a bun to jam into your face when you walked around the attractions.

"These should keep the boss happy; we'll be ready to open tomorrow night." Hagar floored the van as it left the road onto the dirt track through the forest.

"Yes, a good selection of doped up filth." The hairy woman spoke past her thick beard. Her hand was still squelching around in her bikini bottoms. She started to orgasm as the van bounced across the uneven ground, her beard sticking out at an angle as her jaw locked up.

"When we get back I'll have to give you something other than a finger to get you off." The strongman's steroid shrived dick twitching in his at the sound of female masturbation in the seat next to him.

"Why wait for that, we could pull over and fuck in the forest."

"No way, not in this weather. I want to be able to find my dick to fuck. It is far too cold for my arse to be out in that shit."

Gregor

"You can go in my shit if you like. Come on let's fuck in the forest."

"If we are late back the Master will flog me again. You can wait woman."

The bearded lady pulled her slick fingers from her pussy and held them under the strongman's nose. A bump in the road caused them to touch his mouth momentarily. It left behind a stinky smear of her juice. He licked at it, tasting her insides from his top lip.

"Oh, you hairy bitch, you drive me fucking wild." Hagar's tiny dick now as stiff as a thumb tack. "But we have to get this lot back before dawn, on pain of death."

"You're no fun."

"We're not here for fun, after work though," he turned with a toothy smile, "and that arse is getting hollowed out."

He had to fuck her in the arse, years of steroid abuse had withered his manhood to that of a cocktail sausage and it was the only real way she could get any pleasure from it. But even that was a struggle to get through the thicket of hair that covered the majority of her backside.

The forest broke into the clearing where the big top was. Hobo clowns milled around spilling home brew toilet hooch over floppy, hole riddled shoes. Cigarettes hung from their mouths and they huddled around oil drum fires rubbing their grubby fingerless gloved hands together as they coughed their lungs out over each other.

One of the hobos was so plastered he had forgotten to put his dick away in his piss soaked trousers. The bum~clown stumbled into a heap on the ground unconscious and his bladder gave sending a fountain of thick yellow urine into the air and down, over himself. The other hobos just laughed. It wasn't anything they hadn't seen before.

It was a safe bet that he probably voided his bowels as well.

The van slid across the wet ground as Hagar slammed on the anchors. The hobos started to buzz around, looking in through the windows at the selection of fresh junkies in the back. Some of them rubbed at their dirty dicks, hoping for a woman that they could abuse for a few hours while chugging down more toilet booze.

"Get back you scumbags, get away, these have to be taken to the holding cage. There will be no fun for you stinky bums tonight." Hagar pushed his way through the crowed of vagabond clowns and opened the back doors. There was almost a fight as the tramps descended on the junkies, tearing at them and pulling them out.

They writhed around in the mud, still bound like giant grubs as they were pawed over by dirty hands.

"Start dragging them to the cage. If you can manage to get it done quickly I'll leave this one for you." The strongman kicked at a half-naked junkie girl. She screamed a muffled taped up scream past her gag of duct tape and the crowd of hobo clowns roared with delight and started dragging the others into the big top.

Hagar knelt down by the girl. For the merest of moments, he felt a little bad for her. But it didn't matter. If he didn't leave her for the hobos they would only cause trouble trying to get to her in the night.

"I won't lie to you, girly." He looked grim as gestured to the pack of hobos, "but you're in for a rough night."

He stood and threw his arm around his bearded girlfriend's shoulders and pulled her into a head lock. She squealed from the attention now. She was back in some of her gypsy cloths to protect from the ever present storm.

They mooched towards his trailer across the camp. He was smiling and his dick was jutting out like a miniature flagpole in his leopard print speedos. It was anticipating a night of hairy-arsed anal pounding. Hagar looked back to where he had left the junkie girl just in time to see one of the hobos being violently sick next to

Gregor

her as he undid his dirty trousers and climbed between her legs.

Hagar could almost smell the hobo's dick from his trailer door.

He shook his head as he closed the door behind him, "A rough night indeed."

EIGHTEEN

THE BOATMAN WAVED FROM HIS LITTLE CABIN as the boat pulled away, across the black sea into the mist, back down the rocky coast towards the island.

Four of them stood there in the light rain staring at it until it disappeared. Then they all remembered who the fourth member of the party was and looked up at his morbidly painted face.

Johnny stared off into the mist and breathed deeply through his nose. It had been a long while since he had smelt fresh air. The smell of the sea filled his nostrils and his chest expanded stretching the arm restraints to the breaking point.

Pickles stared at his barrel chest expanding and contracting. It made him feel a little bit of acid flavoured sick rise in his throat.

"So what now?" Pickles asked, breaking the silence. He turned to the security guard that was still staring up at the monster Palladuchi.

"Erm?" The guard snapped out of it. "Oh. Well, we have a car stashed in the next village. Like Breen it's as good as deserted. There's only a few vagrants and whatnot, nothing to worry about."

"What then?" Ruby entered.

"We drive to the forest of Breen and hide out until the carnival starts and infiltrate."

"How are we going to do that, we don't have any..." Pickles was cut short by the guard waving a bunch of black and red cards in his face, "... tickets."

"Gotcha covered, matey." Bubbles the guard rummaged through a holdall pulling out two small radios. "Take this just in case the frequency for the boat is written on the side, so if it all goes tits up you can get away... maybe." He turned to look at Johnny with a shudder.

"So I guess we better start hiking then," said Ruby as she slung a bag full of the food she had stolen from the canteen. "Lead the way, boss man."

"Okay, we have to head in that direction." Bubbles pointed towards a road splitting the dense woodland. "Only about fifteen minutes."

"Why the fuck didn't they just leave the car here?" Pickles started off in the direction of the road.

"Because we don't want it to get stolen." Silently he mouthed the word, *idiot.*

"And what's to say that it's not been stolen where you left it?"

"Because it's in a secure location. I told you everything has been planned out."

"Yeah, well there's one thing you can't predict the outcome of."

"So what's that then?" Bubbles crossed his arms.

Pickles turned with a smile. "Whether the big guy's gonna pull your head away from your body when you take off his restraints."

Bubbles looked up at Palladuchi who was now looking down at him. There was something in his eyes that Bubbles didn't like; that look of 'now that is a good idea'.

Nervously Bubbles gestured. "Come on Johnny; let's get out of this weather so we can get that box off your hands." He tried to keep his voice as cautious as he could.

The giant nodded and started lumbering up the trail following the two clowns. Bubble released a small sigh of relief that the monster had actually acknowledged him without incident. He followed the hulking beast down the track.

Ruby stuck tight to Pickles through the sinister looking woodland. Every inch of which was alive with the sound of rain and small creatures as they scurried away from the human invaders. She never much cared for walks in the countryside. There was always something in a bush or up a tree ready to jump out and scare her.

And as for the creepy crawlies, fuck that shit.

She had once been attacked by a stag beetle on a school trip to a hop farm. The thing had buzzed down from a hop silo and got tangled in her hair. Ruby remembered screaming for a good half hour as the teacher was cutting it free with a pair of scissors. She found one of its legs in her hair. It was presumably removed when being hacked free. When she'd gotten home the screaming resumed.

Ruby shuddered to think what was lurking in the foliage in these woods and clung to Pickles arm as he made the call to Gibbon.

Bubbles tugged at Palladuchi's bound arm and questioned, "Who do you think he's calling?" He instantly remembered that he was pulling on the overgrown bicep of a killing machine. If it wasn't for Bubbles' already white painted face Palladuchi would have seen the blood drain away.

The lumbering killer stopped and Bubbles' butthole twitched. The hulk just cocked his head and mimed an overacted 'I don't know' shoulder shrug and continued down the gloomy trail.

Bubbles waited a moment then checked he hadn't shit his pants.

The woods started to thin out until eventually it broke into quaint country lanes. The small village where the car was stashed came into view. Crumbling stone walls lined the lanes all the way down to the derelict slate roofed houses. Most of which were swamped with overgrown bushes and covered with thick ivy.

One building had tree branches jutting out from a broken window where the tree had taken root in the front room and started to grow through the house itself. What a miserable place, gloomy and sinister. The place looked like it was covered in a layer of slime from the rain.

"Just down here, there's a barn behind a pub where the vehicle is hidden. We can rest there until the morning then we'll head to Breen." Bubbles pointed down the lane then turned with a somewhat concerned grimace to Pickles. "And if I can just ask who you were on the phone to? I am under orders not to let our mission be compromised in anyway."

Pickles waved him away and bounded down the lane, the idea of pub lighting up one word in his mind, BOOZE. "Don't worry about it, just a little insurance in case it all gets a bit heavy in the big top." He shouted over his shoulder, "Just a little back up."

"In that case can I point out that I need to know everything that you have planned so I can fit your plan into the plan that the council have planned." Bubbles had confused himself with the words plan and planned and started to count out on his fingers how many times he had said it.

"Please feel free to set fire to your plans and carefully stuff them in your arsehole." Pickles stopped dead outside an ominously gothic looking black stone building covered in ivy with a rotten thatched roof. "Because tonight, my friends, we drink."

Pickles threw his arms up in praise at the building like he had seen an angel descend from the heavens. A painted sign swung in the wind of the upcoming storm with the squeak of metal on metal.

The painting on the sign depicted a witch being burned at the stake by men in black robes holding flaming torches. It read 'The Hag on the Green'.

Gregor

Ruby looked up at the grim sign and felt a little chill run up her spine. "If we're going to stay in this dump I'm going to need a fucking drink."

NINETEEN

WITHIN MOMENTS OF THE FLARE BEING THROWN into the kindling and logs that lay rotting in the fireplace the place was enveloped in heat from a roaring fire. With the addition of a few lit paraffin lamps that hung from the low beamed celling the place almost became cosy.

Bubbles warmed his hands by the fire whilst a content little smile played on his face like a child in front of a buffet of his favourite foods. He turned to see Ruby staring at Johnny who was stooped over at an awkward angle from the cramped conditions.

"Oh, Johnny, please sit down and we can get your box off."

Pickles' head popped up from behind the bar where he was foraging for booze. "You're going to undo him in here?" He was so panicked that his false nose almost went flying across the room.

"Of course, Johnny needs to relax too, you know. We can't have him all tense, and it's a good will gesture." Bubbles crossed the room to where Palladuchi had taken to sitting cross legged. The seated man was still at head height. The clearly scared guard fumbled with first the ankle chains, then the arm restraints.

"Now Johnny, I'm going to take the box off of your hands." Bubbles' hands trembled, the key to the box rattling on the chain. "You can have something to eat. I do believe its jam sponge cake and tangy toms." He looked up at Ruby for confirmation of their supplies and was given a thumbs up. "But you have to promise not to kill anyone. You can do all the killing you like tomorrow night but not any of us... tonight... Just don't kill any of us, okay?"

Palladuchi nodded with a childish almost sarcastic over acted smile and kind face bringing his boxed fists up to meet the key.

"Okay, here we go."

Pickles ducked back down behind the bar and fell on his novelty car horn letting out a single, broken 'HONK' that startled the clown guard just as the key went into the locked box.

"Sorry!" came the voice cowering behind an empty ale barrel under the bar.

There was a click followed by the sound of a mechanism moving inside the box then it fell open into Bubbles' hand. He wasn't ready for the weight and nearly dropped the heavy thing into the maniac's lap. "There, do you feel better Johnny?"

The beast sitting on the floor started to stretch out his giant arms, first rolling his bowling ball sized fists around, then flexing his fingers: open then closed, open then closed. Their joints cracked like someone stamping on tree branches.

He curled up his vast arms, the biceps of which flexed and swelled as he crossed his arms out in from of him then curled them back up into a Mr Universe pose. The light from the fire and the wetness off his skin made his physique look almost mutant; other worldly. It was like he was skinless and formed of just bare copper cables.

Ruby's jaw dropped and her pussy got instantly wet. The tingle inside her came back with vengeance and she realised that it wasn't terror; she was so turned on by the monster. She had never seen such a specimen in her entire life.

Then a voice from behind the bar broke the lust filled silence in the dilapidated lounge bar. "Are we all dead yet?"

A snort of recognition from Palladuchi almost sounded like a laugh and it took all by surprise. Maybe the monster wasn't going to kill them all. Ruby hoped not. At least not before she got the opportunity to find out how beast like he was.

She started to day dream of the thing raping her, ripping her open and crushing her limbs as he roughly entered her, snapping her spine and bending her double. "I need to, erm, find the little girls room."

She got up and headed for the door marked 'toilets' and disappeared inside to masturbate in the dank shithouse.

"BINGO!" Announced Pickles as he emerged from behind the bar with a crate filled with unopened, dusty bottles. "We have two crates of this dubious looking ale and what looks like a few bottles of rum." He smiled, pulling a bottle free from the crate to scan the label. "Should be a good night."

"I don't think drinking now is such a good idea, Mr Pickles."

"Oh, what's wrong with you? We're stuck in this freezing dump in the middle of a storm and you're saying we can't pick up our spirits with a few beers?" He popped the cap of one of the bottles on the edge of the bar. "You want a bottle, big fella?"

Palladuchi clapped and mimed an exaggerated drinking motion then pointed to one of the bottles of rum.

"Good man!"

Pickles came out from behind the bar swigging the out of date ale with a wince and slapped the rum into the waiting mitt of the beast by the fire. His hand engulfed the bottle and he started to chug on it with immediacy until it was half drained. Pickles honked his novelty horn twice as Palladuchi smudged his make-up wiping a dribble of booze from his chin.

"I really don't think this is a good…"

"Relax you. There is nothing like a few stiff ones to get to know your company, takes the edge off." Pickles guzzled the last of the ale and let out a window rattling belch followed by a honk from the horn. "This stuff's a bit rough though. Ah, fuck it." He snapped the top off of another bottle on the fire place and went back to foraging around behind the bar.

The sounds of rummaging through crates and the jangles of bottles were interspersed with the occasional glug, burp and horn honk.

"No Johnny, I don't want you to finish that bottle. We can't have you too drunk on your assignment. Do you remember what happened last time?"

Pickles head popped back up from his investigating. "Last time? You mean to say they have done this sort of thing before?"

"I am not at liberty to divulge that information, Mr Pickles."

"You better tell me what happened on the 'last assignment' or I'm walking away, right now." Pickles slammed his bottle on the bar.

"I am not at liberty to…"

Bubbles was cut short by the sound of Ruby hitting the high notes of orgasm as she bottomed out in the derelict bathroom.

TWENTY

"HOLY SHIT, I'VE HEARD OF HIM." Gibbon paused for a second. "And you're to take him to this circus thing?"

The voice of Pickles sounded shaky on the other end of the phone. "Yeah, then we get to kill a bunch of freaks." The sound of the novelty horn beeped twice on the line.

"So that's why I have a boot full of guns, gotcha."

"Pretty much, look, just meet us outside Breen, okay? Laters."

"No worries, Amigo." Gibbon hung up and threw the phone onto the junk food cluttered dashboard.

"Fuck."

There really wasn't enough beer in the world for this shit but he was loyal, stupidly so. Gibbo wasn't going to just let Ruby stay in that place, stuck with a perverse junkie clown and a serial killing mime artist. He would just have to bite the bullet on this one.

He thought about putting his revolver in his mouth again. He thought about how this would be a really good time to pull the trigger. It's better than the alternative, that's for damn sure. In fact it was much healthier than being punched apart by that fucking nut Palladuchi. And it was much preferred to being raped, murdered *and then* eaten by some pack of deranged circus freaks.

Gibbo hated circus freaks.

He was okay around clowns but it was the others, the oddities that made his skin crawl. The bearded lady, who the fuck wants to see a woman with a fucking beard? The thought made him shudder.

He had once had a fight with some out of work Alligator boy in a bar. He remembered how his clammy, oversized three fingered hand had felt as he tried to strangle the life out of Gibbo. If it hadn't been for a kick in the balls he would have died by the hands of that mutant.

And dwarves, what was the point of dwarves? If there was one thing that creeped Gibbon out the most it was circus midgets. What with their little hands and bulbous heads. He hated how they dressed up like little clowns and were forever getting under your feet. Gibbo despised the way they wore those stupid fucking little bells on their clothes. It was like they were some mutated kitten that would punch you in the balls and run away giggling.

"Fucking monsters," Gibbo caught himself saying it out loud. He thought about the pistol in the glove box again.

No!

No, he wouldn't put it in his mouth again, not this time. The next time he wraps his fingers around the walnut grip of that weapon it will be to squeeze a round of into one of those big faced little people. He was going to paint that fucking big top with the brains of all the little pricks he could shoot. If he was going to go down, it by god would be in a hail of bullets, midget blood and glitter.

The road into Breen was a narrow country lane that was lined with stone walls. Over-hanging trees formed a tunnel that ran all the way to town. Gibbo was forced to drive slowly due to the close proximity of the jagged walls. If anyone was to hop out in front of the car there wouldn't be much he could do to avoid ploughing straight over them.

But eventually the country lane gave way to an open square of dilapidated buildings and boarded up shop fronts.

The place was as good as deserted.

Gibbo parked up on the overgrown village green and scanned the buildings on either side of the car. He imagined the town being quaint many years ago. He saw in his mind's eye the village vicar on his bike waving to the lady at the bakery. He could see the butcher as he was standing proud with arms folded outside his shop. Of course the butcher would have a wink and a ready whistle for any passing customers.

A fruit and veg stall run by two cheeky chappies that knew everything about everyone in the village and would happily turn a blind eye to a schoolboy stealing an apple. The sound of laughter and merriment coming from the pub every night as the sun set and the cider flowed. The fish man selling potted prawns, crab sticks cockles and mussels from an open sided van outside.

Picture perfect.

But not now, not with graffiti on the boards that covered broken glass and smashed up shop fronts. One of the slogans was in letters five feet high in red paint and simply read 'CUNT!' What a shit hole.

Gibbo got out of the car and stretched. The long drive played havoc with his spine. It cracked as he raised his arms and yawned. The air around him stank of the sea mixed with the heady

Gregor

aroma of burning rubbish. It reminded him of a festival he once attended and remembered how drunkenly sick he was at the time.

Then something caught his eye, something moving between the buildings further down the road. What looked like a child covered in dirt peered around from an alleyway then ducked back down knocking over an empty bin as it scurried away.

Gibbo strolled down to where he had spotted the filthy creature. He examined the space between the buildings. The alley itself ran off behind what used to be a metal workshop, judging from the sign over the peeling paint of the sliding doors. At the far end it was gloomy and filled with trash.

Then the thing moved again. The grim covered child wriggled through a hole in one corner of the workshop door.

"Hey!" Gibbo darted down the alley and crouched down to look into the hole in the door. "Wait, where'd you go?"

He started pulling at the loose boards to make the hole big enough to squeeze into. It came away with ease and crumbled in Gibbo's hands from years of neglect and erosion from the sea air.

Inside the workshop was as rubbish filled as the alleyway had been. It was as though someone had emptied dumpster after dumpster of trash over everything. It was all brought together with the strong smell of human shit and burnt rubber.

Gibbo got to his feet and waded through the mountains of garbage into the centre of the beat up old workshop. The place was a museum of dilapidated machinery framed with broken windows and hanging wiring.

The child popped up from a nest of trash in the far corner holding a dirty headless doll tight to its chest.

"Hey, you, have you seen any people around? I'm looking for my friends."

The kid just giggled and the sound seemed to echo around the room, but it wasn't an echo. From all sides additional children had emerged from the piles of rubbish. But these children weren't holding dolls. Lumps of wood, shards of broken glass, bottles and lengths of pipe were what these kids were carrying.

"Fuck," Was all that Gibbo could manage as the bottles started flying his way. The feral children then dived on top of him. Like a pack of rabid spider monkeys they attacked. They were hitting Gibbo with everything they had. All he could do was roll up into a ball on the floor as the weapons bounced off of him.

There was a great crash and the sound of the wooden doors of the workshop getting destroyed. The first of the children was sent flying from a lethal kick between the legs. Another was propelled spinning into the air from a right hook. Another feral child slammed face first into a great metal working lathe, obliterating its dirty face.

Gibbo peered through his arms to see a new feral child being snapped across the knee of a white faced hulk, then an additional one being slammed into the floor like so much dust being beaten from a rug.

Gibbo was yanked to his feet. A friendly face with a red nose and a blue afro smiled as the killing machine put a large case of death to the last of the workshop's children.

"Fuck sake, you do get yourself into some scrapes, mate." Pickles had saved the day and he had brought a monster with him.

TWENTY-ONE

A SQUIRT OF THIN BLOOD MIXED WITH COOKED human fat oozed from the hunk of meat the clown girl was sinking her teeth into. Her face nuzzled at the meat in her hands and her jaw jutted from side to side as she ground down the half cooked flesh.

She was joined by her sisters. They took turns ripping bits of meat off the carved up corpse of dead hobo clown. The meat

Gregor

crackled and fizzed as it turned on a spit over the fire. It was rotated slowly by a naked girl in a pink wig.

The girls were chowing down just outside the camp. They were in a circle of debauchery, under the cover of low hanging trees, at the edge of the forest.

Poor old Knuckles the hobo clown made the mistake of putting his hands in an inappropriate way on one of the girls while drunk. With a smile and a cartwheel he had slapped her ass and exposed his dick. For that he paid the price with a savage display of brutality from the girls.

They had toyed with him at first, chasing him through the woods surrounding the big top with catapults and steel ball bearings. They fired them at him with deadly accuracy to make him change direction and slam into trees. The hobo fell through the bushes before they beat him to death with one of his own floppy shoes. Each of the girls took turns slapping the oversized sole against his head in a frenzy of screams and vaginal masturbation. By the time they had finished, the hobo's head looked like a blood covered medicine ball someone had applied clown make up to.

They ate poor old Knuckles, his dick withered and burnt to a crisp from the fire he slowly rotated over. With a hiss and bright flashes, his fat dripped onto the flames and accelerated the blaze.

"WHAT'S THIS?" A high pitched shout went up that made each girl freeze like a statue. "WHAT IN THE NAME OF ALL THAT'S HOLY DO YOU THINK YOU ARE DOING?"

Mr Thumtumbulous waddled into view through the ring of feeding clown women. He had two other dwarves in tow. He was visibly angry, waving his arms around as he was, and taking swipes at the girls with his walking stick.

"Are you taken leave of your senses?" He screamed. "The show starts in an hour and you have eaten one of the human wranglers. There will be a heavy price for this. You'll have to spend the night in the shit tank."

The girls cowered, mouths still bulging with clown meat. They huddled together, hoping to escape the wrath of their master as he pranced over to the cooking clown on the spit.

"We will have to have the midgets' herd the humans now. It is a shame on account of them tiring so quickly. And what exactly do you suppose will happen if one of the humans tries to escape?" He shook his head at the shivering girls and pointed at his squat companions. "You don't expect the midgets to give chase do you? Why, their legs are nowhere near long enough to stride after startled humans, stupid girls." His stick came down hard onto the thigh of the nearest girl with a slap. She squeaked with pain and rubbed vigorously at the big red welt left by her master.

"Now get back to the big top, there's still plenty to do. People are starting to arrive and I want no more mistakes." Thumtumbulous shook his stick at the girls and hurried them away. They scrambled over each other towards the vast tent and the waiting crowds.

"That's it," he shouted after them, "get working those stalls." He turned back to his dwarf henchmen. "And you two take that remains of this poor fool back to my trailer. I won't waste good meat by leaving it for the foxes."

The dwarves began to dismantle the spit as Thumtumbulous made his way back to the camp. The grounds had already started to bustle with guests and the stalls were lit up with hundreds of coloured bulbs like Christmas trees.

All the naked clown girls were now back at their stations. They were all swanning around and taking money from the endless streams of eager, bloodthirsty customers. They winked and blew kisses at passers-by and slapped at wandering hands that wanted to play with more than the games that were on offer.

Gregor

In a chance to win one of the flesh eating fish that hung in clear plastic bags, punters tried their hand at the piranha stall. They tossed ping pong balls into the goldfish bowls on a stand.

Others threw knives into a rodeo clown that was pinned on a wooden wall. Each body part represented a different prize: stuffed vultures, a painted skull, and teddy bears that were wrapped in used bloody bandages.

A knife flew into the soft flesh of the unwilling clown hanging on the wall. It let out a muffled scream from behind its tight gag. The crowd surrounding the stall roared with delight as the winner was handed a taxidermy statue of a badger smoking a cigar.

Great ladles of a dubious looking meat were being poured into white polystyrene trays over long frankfurter sausages under the modicum of 'greatest chilli dogs in clown town'. No one questioned what was in the thick stew but everyone knew the source of the 'meat'. They dipped hunks of buttered cob into it and ate like gannets.

A line of patrons queued up to throw baseballs, dunking a clown into a waiting vat of viscous liquid. The clown on the seat was tied up and struggling. She was one of the captured women from some supermarket car park. The liquid below stank of acid. It was waiting to dissolve the flesh from her bones if a ball found its mark.

Thumtumbulous was pleased. The crowd was swelling and the big top was more than ready to go. It would be the greatest spectacle of torture and humiliation ever to be put on under canvas. He rubbed his hands together with greedy delight at the thought of counting all that money. He'd do it in the comfort of his trailer, later that night, as he tucked into a roast hobo clown sandwich.

A dwarf henchman appeared from under the skirt of the big top wall and toddled over with news. "Everything is ready, master.

We are all just waiting for you to give the okay and we can get started." He wiped a layer of sweat off his head from the brisk jog. "Shouldn't you be getting ready, master?"

Mr Thumtumbulous waved the sweaty midget away. "You know the rules, Plato old friend. The longer you make them wait, the more money they'll spend."

Still rubbing his hands, he let out a tiny cackle of greed. Mr Thumtumbulous made his way back to his trailer. He had to apply his makeup for the show.

TWENTY-TWO

"AH, POOR BABY," Ruby poked at Gibbo's bandaged head, right on the red dot of blood that had seeped through the gauze.

"Fuck off, woman." Gibbo swatted her hand away as the pain from the prod buzzed through his skull. "Goddamn those fucking kids! Man, if it wasn't for El Giganto over there I thought I was done for sure." He pointed over at Johnny Palladuchi. He was wrapping his hands in fresh white tape.

"Grow up for fuck sake." Pickles rummaged in the back of the car for his bag. He was glad to not be wedged in the back with two other guys. Especially considering that one of the guys was nearly as big as the car itself. "You got the shit kicked into you by children. We saved your ass and Ruby patched you up. Other than that gash on your head you'll be fine. The scars will be mostly mental." His voice was thick with sarcasm.

Gibbo rubbed at his sore head. "So what's the plan?"

"Glad you asked." Pickles popped out from the car and slammed the door. "You hang back with the giant and his handler while me and Ruby pose as patrons and infiltrate the big top. We'll 'fact find' first. Next we're supposed to send in slugger over there, but fuck that noise! Why should he have all the fun?" Pickles pulled out a flare gun and waggled it at Gibbo. "I give the signal and you lot come in all guns blazing. We kill every last freak we can find, then make our way back to the council with the midget's corpse they want so badly. We'll just say it all went tits up and we had to fight our way out. If the big man gets a little out of his pram we'll be forced to blow his head off with that bomb collar thingy. The plan is so simple it can't fail."

"I like it. I could do with killing something tonight." Gibbo recalled every last blow the children had thrown down on him. He felt he was owed a little payback.

"Don't you mean as long as it's not a gang of kids wanting to kick your flabby arse again, right?" Ruby laughed in Gibbo's face.

"Fuck you." He extended a fat middle finger bruised from trying to block a 2x4 swung by a feral child.

"Ladies, ladies, ever heard of a thing called team work?" Pickles honked his novelty horn twice. "Now let's get this show on the road. Bubbles, we're hitting bricks. See you later Johnny."

"Later on," Bubbles waved back. Johnny just nodded and flexed his hands under the new layer of tape. He still gave Pickles the creeps. He didn't dare show it as he and Ruby set off down the track into the forest.

A light glowed over the top of the trees from deep in the wood. The sounds from the big top floated through the air. A giant out of key mechanical pipe organ belched out creepy music. It accompanied the screams of people on rickety fairground rides.

Everywhere was the smells of popcorn, stale beer and sideshow chilli dogs. The drone of massive diesel generators rumbled thunder beneath their feet as they got closer to the main gate.

A dwarf manned the booth. He was protected from both the elements and rowdy customers by a sheet of glass. The booth had a slot for the exchange of cash for tickets. The little chap was eating a banana and dressed like a pantomime genie. He appeared clearly fed up as Ruby and Pickles approached.

"Welcome to the Big Top O'Pain where nightmares become reality. Do you require a guest pass, fun fair pass or do you have tickets?" He spoke with a lump of the fruit jutting out from the corner of his mouth.

Pickles whipped out the complimentary tickets. "We have tickets my friend, and just what time does the show start?" Pickles honked on his horn and shot the dwarf a cheeky smile.

Still with a face like thunder like he had seen it all before he replied, "The big top opens in half an hour for patrons and the show starts in forty five." He stamped a hole in each of the tickets with a silver punch and handed them back through the glass. "Enjoy the show... or whatever."

Pickles nodded and still smiling returned with, "Why thank you so much, you miserable little bastard."

The dwarf just shrugged off the insult.

"I want one of those chilli dogs and a beer." Ruby sounded like a child as she hung from Pickle's arm. "And I want you to win me one of those balloon animals." She pointed to the knife throwing stall and a selection of deformed balloon creatures.

Pickles eyed up the victim pinned to the back board and nodded. "Sure, who says we can't have a little fun while we're on our fact finding mission."

The two of them approached the stall where a naked clown girl was fondling an oversized throwing knife. She shot a wink to Pickles as he neared the counter.

"I like your nose," she said pointing the blade at the red bulb on his face, "You feel lucky with that big old nose, Mr?"

"I'll chance an arm, my dear." The sleaze of trying not to sound like he was flirting poured from him as the girl handed him the first of three knives.

The knife was heavy. Pickles weighed it up as he eyed his target. It wriggled on the back wall. With an almighty swing he let fly with his first effort. It stuck in the wall with a thud just below the prone clown's left arm.

"Not bad." The naked clown girl giggled. "But not great. You're going to have to throw better than that if you want to win something for your skank." She sneered at ruby.

"Hey, watch your tongue, bitch." Ruby edged forward.

"Come on now, it's just a game." The second of the blades thudded into the wall just above the prone clown's head that gave out a whine of relief, "Arse!"

"Last one, big nose." The clown girl kissed the tip of the last of the knives and handed it over.

"Just for luck, right?" asked Pickles. He lined up the blade and pulled his arm back. He closed one eye to get a better range, and then Pickles let it fly. The knife was in the soft part of the clown on the wall's belly as soon as it left his hand. It was thrown with such force it'd gone straight through. The tip was stuck in the back board.

"WOOOOOOO!" Pickles and Ruby danced with delight as the clown girl pulled the blade from the clown target's gut. From behind the paper Mache mash, the victim coughed out a jet of blood from its nose and slumped forward.

"What do I win, what do I win?" Pickles was lit up like a Christmas tree. He honked his horn and grabbed at Ruby's arse. Ruby slapped his hands away and pointed to the prizes hanging from a rack overhead.

"That one, that one! I want the deformed giraffe."

The clown girl hooked it down by using a stick with a bent nail in the top. She dutifully handed over the gross balloon animal. "That also doubles as a hat." She said with a level of contempt.

Just then a crackle of static came over the big tops PA system and a squeaky voice echoed around the fair ground: "The show will be starting soon ladies and gentlemen! All ye, all ye, in come free! So roll on up, for the show starts in five minutes!"

"I guess we better get to our seats then Roobs." Pickles pointed over to the slowly shuffling queue of patrons making their way into the big top through the main gate. Pickles and Ruby joined the chain gang and with the rest of the crowd made their way into the gloom of the tent.

TWENTY-THREE

THE LIGHTS IN THE TENT DROPPED. The clamour of patrons anxiously waiting in their seats fell to a low hum of mumbles and whoops.

The place had become a pitch dark bee hive.

Pickles and Ruby fidgeted on the hard plastic bench. They stuffed their faces with popcorn, deep-fried corn mash covered hot dogs, cheese covered nachos, and chilli fries. The snacks were bought from a visibly retarded clown that came around with a huge tray.

Through the dark a strobe light began to flash high up in the roof and the tent was filled with the sounds of thunder through a shoddy PA system. A high pitched squeak of a voice crackled over the top of the theatre grade backing track of a child's toy piano:

"Boys and girls of all ages, welcome to the Big Top O' Pain."

"Here we go, here we go!" Pickles squeezed Ruby's thigh with his grease covered mitt.

"You will thrill at the spectacle of live death! Gasp with amazement at the horrific torture and wow at the threshold of the human body." The high squeak turned into a sinister laughter, "Let the show begin!"

The house lights burst through the tent.

Hobo clowns and naked girls with coloured hair darted around the centre ring, back flipping and tumbling and juggling with bright red balls. Overhead a group of naked men swung through the sky on corpses roped up to form a macabre trapeze. The three flying acrobats' faces were obscured with cloth potato sacks. Around their necks were severed hangman's nooses. Each acrobat flipped over and crossed each other's path, landing effortlessly on small platforms attached to the main poles of the vast tent.

A small steam powered wagon chugged into the centre of the ring looking like a big black birthday cake. A tiny ring master appeared from the top of it, arms aloft in triumph.

"That's the little fucker the council wants," spat Pickles through a mouthful of fries as he pointed enthusiastically.

The little man spoke into a microphone, "Boys and girls, way above us are the Flying Bigoli Brothers! Watch now as they attempt the bloody, the maniacal, the visceral... Ching Wang's dancing swords of death!"

One of the brothers set off through the air on his corpse swing while the other two produced vicious looking swords from behind their backs. Then they too swung off over the crowd.

It was like a morbid ballet the way the acrobats glided and spun effortlessly through the air. Each one holding on one handed as they swung their swords and criss-crossed each other. Their dicks were slapping all about in the wind all the while.

The first brother flung himself into a backflip above his cadaver swing and the other two closed in on the hanging body. Their swords found their mark. They split the corpse cleanly down the middle and as brother one fell he caught the ankles of each spit piece. The three of them were splattered with gore as they swung back to the safety of the platforms.

The crowd gasped. They burst into rapturous applause as the contents of the stiff splashed down onto the front row of patrons. It covered at least five of them in guts and rotten blood.

There was even more applause as two clearly drunk hobo clowns theatrically mopped up the mess from the guests with white towels.

The crowd fell about with laughter at their buffoonery.

Another clown ran across the ring with a bucket. He made out like he was going to throw it over the messy patrons in the front row. The other hobos dived for cover. Then picking his victim the clown let fly. But it wasn't glitter that flew out from the bucket. Rather some sort of highly corrosive liquid. It doused a middle aged woman who was still wiping the gore from her eyes with a clown towel. The liquid sizzled the second it hit her skin and she let out a blood curdling scream as the rest of the crowd around her backed away in fright.

She clawed at her face, ripping away great smouldering chunks with her melting hands. Then she slumped back into her seat a pile of slowly dissolving, screaming goo.

Above, the Bigoli took a bow and waved their swords in the air. Ruby tugged at Pickles' shirt, her face lit up like a child at Christmas. "This is the greatest thing I have ever seen. I can smell that woman melting and everything."

Pickles was glued himself and squeezed harder on Ruby's leg. "I know. It's almost a shame we to have to break up this party."

Ruby pointed at the seat where the puddle of a woman squelched and spat, "Oh, not yet, let's see what happens next." Her face was like a pug that had been told off: all big eyes and grumpy mouth.

"Okay, but after I finish these nachos I'm setting off the flare gun." Pickles shoved a handful of the oozing chips into his face as a fanfare sounded over the PA.

The tiny ring master trundled around the ring on his steam powered birthday cake screeching into the mic.

"Now that was a display of wonder?! Did you enjoy the crowd participation, boys and girls?" The crowd lit up and clapped, rumbling the benches with stamping feet.

"And now we have an act where the worlds of mysticism and depravity collide head on... introducing the Great Alfabeto!"

A puff of smoke, a clap of amateur dramatics club grade thunder and the Great Alfabeto stood proud in the centre ring. Stage hands scurried around as the thin man with white hair and red velvet lined cape pranced waving his hands. He was pulling cards out of the air and firing them into the crowd like ninja throwing stars.

The stage hands wheeled out a large wooden frame with chains hanging from it to a table. Evil looking meat hooks were waiting at each end. They glistened like they'd been rubbed with baby oil. On the table a woman was strapped down. Her eyes were sewn shut with bandages and thick black fishing wire. From the look on her face she'd been heavily sedated. Her head rocked from side to side, and she was drooling from the corners of her mouth.

Around the table Alfabeto's insanely attractive assistant Pizazz strutted all leggy, tits and teeth wrapped in a blue sequin dress that left little to the imagination. A huge water lily in her purple bobbed hair, she waved to the crowd and they all waved back.

Pickles was paying particular attention to her.

The magician made his way to the prone woman on the table. He whipped off his cape and handed it to his assistant who just threw it under the table.

Alfabeto waggled a finger at her in a 'NO, NO, NO' motion. Pizazz shrugged and pulled the cape back out. She began folding it properly. It was all adding to the theatrics. The magician nodded and waved but as his back was turned the assistant booted it back under the table.

The crowd laughed and clapped, for it was all very funny.

Pizazz handed the first of the hooks to the Great Alfabeto. He held it aloft for all to see then snatched it down to begin threading it through the fat meat of the prone woman's thigh. It squeaked as the skin broke. It popped through the other side with ease.

The next hook went through the flesh of the under arm just as easily. Next was her plump belly, then her neck, and another two through the opposite leg and arm. Two more: one through each flabby buttock and one each through the hands. The crowd gasped with the crunching of bones as the magician forced them through. The last went through the flesh of her cheeks, and through her mouth. The victim's tongue was flopping out like an old dog's trying to cool down.

With the woman hooked up to the frame, Pizazz took a bow and left through the back of the tent as the magician pranced and released the straps holding the poor victim down. He danced up to the front of the crowd and clapped three times. The frame sprung apart hoisting the woman upright into a standing position on the table.

The crowd was taken aback with the speed of the contraption.

Then with another set of claps there was a puff of smoke from the table and the contraption ripped the drugged woman into several pieces sending lumps of flesh and blood in every direction. When the smoke cleared the lovely Pizazz was standing proud with one hand in the air and one hand on her hip, her tits and arse jutting in opposite directions like a gymnast after landing a spring. She was covered in head to toe in the ripped up woman's gore. Tiny bits of meat were stuck in between the sequins of her dress. Her hair was slick with blood. The white lily was now a bright pink from the woman's innards.

The crowd roared and stood in a mass standing ovation. Pickles had seen enough.

"Well I guess that's going to have to be the show stopper." He sucked the last of the nacho cheese from his fingers and raised the flare gun.

TWENTY–FOUR

GIBBO SAT IN THE DRIVER'S SEAT OF HIS CAR, his legs out through the open door. He was smoking and watching how Bubbles was so nervous around Jonny Palladuchi.

The big man was sat cross legged on the ground and every time he moved his hands or his head Bubbles flinched.

No one spoke.

His gun was in his lap again.

He could so easily back out of this with one squeeze of the trigger but he figured he could do with a little death killing.

A little payback for his bandaged head.

A little much needed release.

The silence was killing him so he turned to switch on the radio. Some oldies started to honk out of the speakers. How he hated the 80's and all its trappings but some of the music was okay. Luckily it was the Fine Young Cannibals with Jonny Come Home.

Then someone made the seated giant prick up his ears and Gibbo realised he was being stared at. He didn't want to make eye contact and thought he would break the ice with some light conversation with the monsters handler but all he could come up with was...

"How much does that big mother fucker eat anyhow?"

Palladuchi's blank expression turned to a scowl that made Gibbo's sphincter twitch just as a flash of green light followed by a bang lit up the sky over the trees.

Bubbles snapped to attention. "That looks like our mark. Are you ready to beat on some circus freaks, Jonny?"

The hulk climbed to his feet. A smile crossed his wide face and he slammed a fist into his opposite hand with a sound like a tree snapping.

"Well what are you two waiting for?" Gibbo took his gun and placed it on the dash and started the car. "Let's go kill some fucking midgets!"

The car ripped through the trees on the dirt track towards the big top its high beams flashing like a strobe light from all the dips and potholes on the path. Gibbo gripped the wheel tight. One flick of the wrist and they would be face planting a tree.

But then the track opened up and the carnival was in view. There were a handful of people still playing the sideshow games. Trying to dunk the clown in the vat of acid, throwing knives into struggling victims pinned to walls.

The car made the main gate kiosk where the miserable banana eating dwarf inside just had time to look up as the vehicle crashed through the booth and into the carnival.

The look on his face for that split second was priceless; a mix of confusion and terror, pure horror with a mouthful of fruit. It made Gibbo's sphincter twitch in a different way and the sensation made him burst out in hysterics.

"DIE YOU FREAK SACKS OF SHIT!"

The naked clown girl on the knife throwing stall was a little luckier and managed to dart out of the way of the marauding vehicle as it came to a stop within the back wall of the stand. Two of the three bound up living targets were taken clean out by the car in

Gregor

the collision. The third was sent up in the air. It ended landing face down in the mud in front of the stall.

Gibbo was the first out of the car with his pistol poised. The clown girl was getting to her feet and grabbing for one of the throwing knives.

"You shouldn't have done that mister, now you're for it. NOW YOU'RE FOR IT!"

He lowered the gun and reached for the passenger door handle. "You're up slugger."

The door swung open and Jonny Palladuchi squeezed out from the back seat. The clown girl paused for a moment to take in the size of the beast. For a second she wondered how big his dick was before pouncing into attack mode. The knife was up and she was screaming.

The clown girl was met with a neck snapping punch that not only stopped the banshee like howl but folded her head back like an envelope flap. Before she had even hit the ground more of the naked clown girls sprung from behind their stalls and leapt at the giant killing machine.

Jonny swatted at them sending some flying, broken and crumpled. Somehow others managed to get past the great swinging fists. Those that made it climbed over him like naked sexy assed spider monkeys. They were all scratching and biting as Jonny fought them off.

"It looks like our boy has his hands full with those bitches." Bubbles appeared from the other side of the car. "Let's get into the tent and light this fucking fire."

"I'm down with that." Gibbo let off a shot to a clown girl gearing up to stick a knife into the beast Jonny's back. The hollow point slug hit her square in the side of the head. The bullet burst out the other side, sending her green afro wig spinning off. It was filled to capacity with splintered skull and brain matter.

Gibbo couldn't tell from the melee but he was sure that the monster gave him a nod of appreciation. But he couldn't wallow in it as he and Bubbles had to enter the tent.

Behind the entrance flap of the big top they were met with a bizarre sight. Ruby was wrestling on the ground with a blood covered girl in a sequin dress, both of whom were screaming the words "fucking bitch, fucking bitch" at each other. Pickles was running after a little man in a top hat and tails on a weird looking steam engine while being chased by drunken hobo clowns. All the while the crowd around the main ring cheered at them and clapped. They thought it was all part of the show.

"We found the party." Gibbo couldn't believe his eyes and started laughing again.

"Let's get ourselves a drink." Bubbles ran screaming into the main ring shooting at anything with a painted face while Gibbo stood rooted trying to work out what he meant.

"A drink?" He scratched his head with his pistol. "That makes no fucking sense."

Not giving it a second thought he too ran into the ring shooting at clowns as he made his way over to Ruby.

Some of the crowd now realised that this was not part of the show. They began to scream and ran towards the exits. Others climbed over the hay bales separating the stands from the ring to fight with the intruders that had interrupted their entertainment. Bubbles decided it was time to start firing indiscriminately into the surging masses, laughing all the while. He was a man possessed as the blood lust took over, twisting his face up to that of a gore frenzied mad man.

Bodies tumbled as Bubbles opened up his machine gun into the oncoming traffic of patrons. He sent corpses to the ground one after another.

Bubbles had become chaos.

Gregor

Gibbo had to duck out of the way of the hail of bullets to get to Ruby who was now straddling the magician's assistant. She had two handfuls of hair pounding her head into the ground.

"Shazam your way out of this, bitch." Ruby was intent on pummelling the sequin clad girl's brains out of her ears and Gibbo struggled to pull her off. When he did the still squirming Ruby had clumps of ripped out purple hair in each hand.

Pizazz shuddered with rage on the floor, coughing out blood. Her nose was stowed in from Ruby's brutal attack. "My face, what have you done to my face?"

"Oh shut up about your fucking face." Gibbo let his pistol finish the conversation. The bullet entered the assistant's face through her chin. It ruptured as it shattered through the bone causing all the fragments to exit through her soft throat like a claymore mine. Her neck pulsed then burst. Clearly, it would be her final show.

A puff of smoke sent Gibbo and Ruby crashing to the ground as the Great Alfabeto sprang at them. His fingernails had extended and seemed to be made of metal. He hissed at the pair and raised his arms like a theatrical vampire and moved in for the kill.

Then his genital area exploded.

A splash of red, the slug burst out from his butthole with a trail of blood and shit. The magician had a look of total shock and let out an almost silent, high pitched scream that could shatter glass. He looked up to see Bubbles standing there, his smoking machine gun still pointing at what used to be his balls.

Alfabeto dropped to his knees, let out one last "abracadabra" with raised eyebrows and a wave of his hand then slumped face down into the sawdust covered ground. His ass was high in the air exposing the gruesome exit wound for the entire world to see.

Ruby looked up at their saviour. "I can't believe you shot a magician in the dick?"

"That's nothing; I once punched a disabled woman in a library." And with that Bubbles continued his rampage through the mass of hobo clowns.

Ruby and Gibbo got to their feet and dusted themselves down. "You okay, baby girl?"

"Yeah I'm good, is my make-up okay?"

"It's pretty fucked up." Gibbo looked grim.

"Fucking bitch." Ruby stamped on what was left of the magician's assistant's face. "Oh well, no time to sort it out, better…"

She was cut short with Gibbo bursting into a fit of hysterical laughter and pointing. "Oh my fucking lord, check that out."

"What?" Ruby tuned to see that Pickles had climbed on to the back of the steam powered buggy and was being violently strangled by the dwarf ring master. His tongue was sticking way out and his arms were waving madly in the air.

She started laughing too. "I guess we better help him out."

TWENTY–FIVE

THE HORN IN HIS HAND CRASHED INTO THE SIDE of the midget's head with a distorted 'HONK' as it connected.

The little man's hat flew off. He fell back into the steam engine's compartment. The one he had emerged from at the start of the show

Pickles jumped in after the fallen dwarf. He proceeded to punch the wee ring master in the face over and over with the horn that was still clenched tight in his fist. Every 'HONK' hit a different note. With each blow the horn caved in, becoming more and more dented and out of shape from the pummelling.

"Oh you little bastard, I've fucking had it with you."

HONK, HONK, HONK, HONK, HONK.

With one last huge 'HONK' the midget was put to sleep.

Gregor

Pickles' blue afro popped out of the top of the steam engine in time to see the strong man about to slam into the wagon. His shoulder down, he threw himself into it crumpling the front of it, stopping it dead. It sent the triumphant clown inside flying out. Pickles landed hard and flipped over twice until he came to a stop against the hay bales that surrounded the ring.

Ruby and Gibbo darted over to pick the busted clown up. Pickles was dazed but got to his feet and squeezed the bulb on his crooked horn. It gave out a defeated squeak.

"Well, now we have to deal with this fat sack of shit." Pickles wiped away a dribble of blood from his mouth and raised his fist… then he started to laugh.

"What's the joke, funny man?" The strong man flexed his tits as he stalked towards them.

"Oh, it's really nothing," Pickles continued to laugh and was joined in the merriment by Ruby and Gibbo.

The strong man stopped in his tracks. "So what's so damn funny?"

"Oh, really nothing," Pickles wiped the tears from his cheek, "Just the four hundred pound nightmare we lovingly call Jonny Palladuchi."

"Who the fuck is Jonny Palla…"

A huge finger attached to a bowling ball sized bloody tape wrapped hand tapped the strong man on the shoulder. The strong man turned to face a wall of scratched and bitten meat, raised veins and pulsing muscle.

Jonny crabbed in front of the smaller man, his arms looking like they were going to split open from the surging flesh underneath and the space around him seemed to bend. The strong man filled his leopard print speedos with all the excretions a bladder and bowel could produce.

Then the punch came.

It connected to the strongman's jaw with the sound of a cannon firing. It spun his head around 180 to face the three standing stunned behind him. All three took a step back and exclaimed "WHOA" at the same time.

Palladuchi proceeded to pick the strong man up by his twisted neck and his balls. He raised the strong man up over his head then brought him down. Jonny snapped him like a dry branch over his knee just as a bearded woman in gypsy clothing stuck a knife in Jonny's back.

It did little to nothing in the way of slowing the big man down. Jonny grabbed at the woman's long whiskered chin and flung her in the air, whipping her like a wet towel. The skin of her face gave with the force of the action and she was sent a good thirty feet across the ring screaming while the scalped beard remained in Palladuchi's massive mitt. It hung from his fist, a flap of skin holding on by a good length of beard.

Jonny Palladuchi smiled and performed a surfer style muscle flex in the fashion of the mime artist that he accompanied with a sarcastic pout of his bottom lip.

"That was fucking brutal." Ruby felt a twitch between her legs for the big man but snapped pout of it pretty fast remembering he was an insane killing machine.

"Never mind that shit. That little fucker is getting away." Gibbo was pointing at the tiny ring master waddling towards the entrance flap in the tent.

"I need that fucker's corpse." Pickles bolted after the still dazed dwarf honking his deformed clown's horn with every other step. The others followed with Jonny hanging back to stare at the chin scalp in his hands. He sniffed at it before poking his tongue out to taste a little of the blood that oozed off of it.

Outside it was a bloodbath. Destroyed clown girls as naked as the day as they were born littered the carnival in various states of

Gregor

broken. The walls of all the booths were splattered with blood and coloured wigs were dotted all over the place.

Pickles was surprised how far the little man had gotten. He was just through the caved in ticket booth and on his way down the track.

"I'll take care of the little shit-bag." Gibbo raised his pistol.

"Wait," Pickles pushed the gun away, "I got this." He reached down for one of the naked clown girls' throwing blades and drew it back over his shoulder. He shut one eye and remembered how his dick had stiffened a little in his shorts when the clown girl had called him big nose. He remembered the way she had winked at him and kissed the tip of the blade. He remembered how her head had snapped back from the killer Jonny's fist.

The knife flew through the air at lightning speed and hit the little man in the back of the head with a slap. He staggered for a moment and flopped face down in the dirt. He was still for a moment. Then he got back to his feet. He tried to reach for the blade sticking out of his skull but his arms were just not long enough.

He fell to his weird little knees and his arms went limp at his side. His head flopped back from the weight of the substantial knife.

"WOOOOOOOOOOO, FUCKING BULL'S EYE!" Pickles jumped for joy and went bounding over to confirm his kill. He stopped dead and his hands came up to his mouth with glee at what he saw. "Hey you guys, come check this out! It hit him so hard one of his eyes has popped out."

Sure enough when the others got there the little fellow's right eye was hanging out. Blood poured from his nose and covered the front of his micro ringmaster's costume.

"That's pretty gross." Bubbles wiped away some saliva from his mouth and held back the need to throw up.

"Yeah right, coming from Rambo over here," Gibbo slapped him across the back. "And just what happened to you in there, psycho, get a bit trigger happy did we?"

"That was different."

"In what way?" Ruby crossed her arms.

"Look, fuck off okay? So what I got a bit carried away." Bubbles was blushing.

"Carried away?" Gibbo laughed the comment off.

"I think we have a more pressing problem at this time."

"Like what?"

"Well the car's fucked. How are we meant to get back to the boat?"

Pickles snapped his fingers. "I have an idea, you lot wait here." He went running back into the tent and a moment later the chugging of the steam powered engine of the dwarf's cart could be heard. It chuntered out from the flap and Pickles stood triumphant on top of the contraption.

It slowed to a halt and Pickles hopped down.

"Well this should get us to the boat and I think it might be a good idea to start some fires. We could use that stick of dynamite too, but I think we might have a bit of a bigger problem." He looked back at the tent and raised his aviators. "Jonny's gone."

TWENTY–SIX

"WHAT ARE YOU TRYING TO TELL ME? That everyone is now dead, including one of the most violent men on the planet?" Patches Theobald's voice was a burnt out croak from rage, slamming both hands on the expansive table in the council chamber.

"Pretty much," Pickles scratched deep in his blue afro and hid behind his mirrored shades, "I mean he just went nuts and got some insane blood boner. It was quite something and there really was no stopping the guy."

Gregor

"And you are sure he is dead?" Theobald smelt a rat and leaned in to get a better sniff of it.

"Oh, most definitely, your honour. He started to fuck about with that collar thing and his head just exploded. It was pretty funny." He smirked over the top of his shades. Bubbles and Ruby tried not to laugh as they stood quietly behind the lying clown.

"And you can vouch for this, agent Bubbles?" The high councillor raised an eyebrow.

"Yes sir, I can validate everything this clown stated, including the way he saved my life. He also defeated a gang of naked funny girls single handed and then he brought down the evil midget Thumtumbulous, sir." Bubbles shot Pickles a look. Pickles had hammed up his account of what had happened, but they had all agreed to stick with the story and follow his lead.

"Very well, we are not happy with the situation but you have at least brought us the body of that insidious dwarf." Patches Theobald stood and made for the door behind him.

"Just a last word before you go, your majesty." Pickles coughed into his hand.

"Well, what is it, man?"

"When are you cock suckers gonna give me my money?"

SEVERAL MILES AWAY, across the sea, just outside the town of Breen there smoulders the remains of the black carnival. The area was as good as a bomb site with next to nothing left standing.

The stick of dynamite had packed more than a hefty punch on the wooden stalls and canvas tent. The sideshow booths and amusements became nothing but splintered matchwood. The remains of cheap stuffed animals lay deformed and melted from the blast all over the ground.

What hobo clowns that were still left alive finished off the dying with hammers. They piled the remains onto the fires then took what they could and left in a caravan of their own. They would start over, anywhere that would have them and their strange ways. Somewhere down the road they would find work but for now they had to put as much ground between then and the wasted carnival site as was possible. The air was thick with the stink of burning flesh and well overdone popcorn.

As good a job as the hobos had done of clearing the last of the bodies away they had missed someone. He was crawling his way out from a wrecked animal cage. A strip of yellow balloon rubber was still hanging from the tip of his penis.

Chris was still alive.

"I CAN'T BELIEVE I HAD TO AGREE with all that bullshit." Bubbles was leading Ruby and Pickles through the clown prison. "Single handily taking out a pack of funny girls? Seriously, the most you did was to get strangled by a midget."

"Hey, I had to beef the story up a bit and besides, he went for it. We are all getting paid. Gibbo gets paid, Ruby gets paid and most of all I get paid. That means I get to go see that bitch Queen Dominic and score me a big old bag of whatever the fuck the kids are into these days. I plan to spend the next month in another dimension."

"Good to see you have some life goals and that you included me in the payment plan." Ruby shoved her elbow into the clown's ribs.

"Hey, never let it be said I don't look after my peoples."

Pickles honked his dented up horn twice.

CHRIS STAGGERED TO HIS FEET, the chain still around his wrists dragging a shattered piece of wood behind him. He was naked and dazed but free of the cage and the hellish circus that had him captive. The air around him was acrid with smoke as the winds

G r e g o r

picked up through the tattered tent. The storm was starting up again and the spots of rain on Chris's face pulled him back into reality.

The last thing he could remember was one of those devil clown women taking a piss over him before the cage he was in exploded and rolled over. Chris vaguely recalled everything going rather dark and quiet.

But now he was out and dragging his plank down the dirt-track into the woods. There just had to be a town or something nearby, he was sure. Somewhere there had to be a place where he could call someone for help. He just had to get the hell out of this nightmare.

The rain rattled through the trees. The forest was alive once more as the wind whipped through branches that were strained with creaks and cracks. The sky grew dark and the ominous rumbles of distant thunder brought the first of the heavy rain.

Chris for a moment stopped. He thought he saw something. One of those fucking clowns in the trees looking at him. His blood froze. He stumbled forward, his movements laboured by the wood that was chained to his wrists. He looked back to where he thought he saw the clown in the forest.

Nothing.

He must have imagined it, his mind playing tricks. With all he had gone through he wondered if he would ever be the same again. He sighed with relief and continued down the track.

He didn't even care that the popped balloon was still hanging from his urethra.

THROUGH THE TREES HE WATCHED CHRIS STRUGGLE his way down the trail. He had a white panted face with a single red tear under his left eye. A mass of muscle and murderous rage flexed and twisted as he breathed deeply. A fist the size of a bowling ball rolled up white-knuckle tight. The other hand was naught but a gory stump from successfully ripping off his bomb collar.

Jonny Palladuchi spat saliva on the nubbin, lapping at the blood from his wound like a wild animal.

All the while eying little Chris with bad intent.

END.

<u>ABOUT THE AUTHOR:</u>

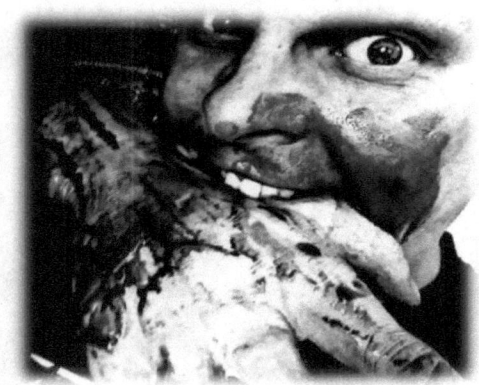

GREGOR COLE works out of Kent (the garden of England) in the UK spending most of his free time scribbling away in the gloom and watching classic horror.

He sharpens the knives of his craft on a diet of tea, biscuits and lemon loaf cake, constantly waiting for the postman to deliver his weekly selection of gore films and Bizarro literature.

Also available from ~<u>MorbidbookS</u>~
In Print & Kindle Editions. Available at Amazon.com,
CreateSpace.com and Barnes&Noble online:
~click on image for HYPERLINK~

~ **It wasn't long before the contents of his mysterious** trunk were revealed to her. It was true, they were props, and some of them might even have been used in the circus. Whips and crops, handcuffs, gags and blindfolds. He applied each of them to her liberally and with sadistic abandon. She took to each of them and craved more. This was the other side of Salero, the one he hid, the dark side. Publically, the man loved and craved the laughter and applause of children. But as much as he craved the laughter of children, he also craved the cries and screams of women as they submitted to his own particular brand of sadism. He wielded a whip better than any lion tamer in the business. It thrilled him to watch the firm young flesh of a woman writhe and twist in delicious agony as his ropes bit deeply into them and his crops left myriads of latticework markings on their bodies. Their anguish was his delight.

~**Rae is her name.** Our support group of embittered and most likely deranged women are going to kidnap, torture, disembowel and finally kill the woman who has ruined all our lives. As foul and as grotesque as she is, she acts like she's Queen of the Bean. Rae, her buck-tooth grin and rosy cheeks of middle age acne reflected winter sun. Straw-like blonde hair obscured by the veil and tiara she enjoyed parading around in. She walked past our window with sickening confidence oblivious to us and our weak tea. Rae. Everything was always about Rae. Was she a princess today, or was she a bride? We wished we could be that delusional and walk around with an air of not giving a damn. Rae believes she is above the pain she has caused. Beyond the whimpering of her victims. Out of reach of vengeance. Our support group of women do not agree. Judgement day is here for Rae.

~Maybe it had started when he was at university.

He had a girlfriend in his final year that had gotten him into some weird stuff sexually then she left him for a guy with a bigger cock. The other guy was some gay looking chump with muscles and a tattoo; the pair had died in a car accident and Brian took a dump on their graves after each of their funerals. Fuck the both of them.

But after she had left him he needed to fill the void of the newfound enjoyment of sickening sexual practices. Brain had purchased one of those 'real life' sex dolls online. Boy did the thing look real; you could bend it into any position and it came armed with enormous tits, willing mouth and a supposedly real feel pussy and anus. The packaging said to 'just add lubricant' but there was a problem. There was something missing; the smells, the tastes and the feel of real skin. You can't emulate that. So Brian set out to attempt to build a real life sex toy made from real life people.

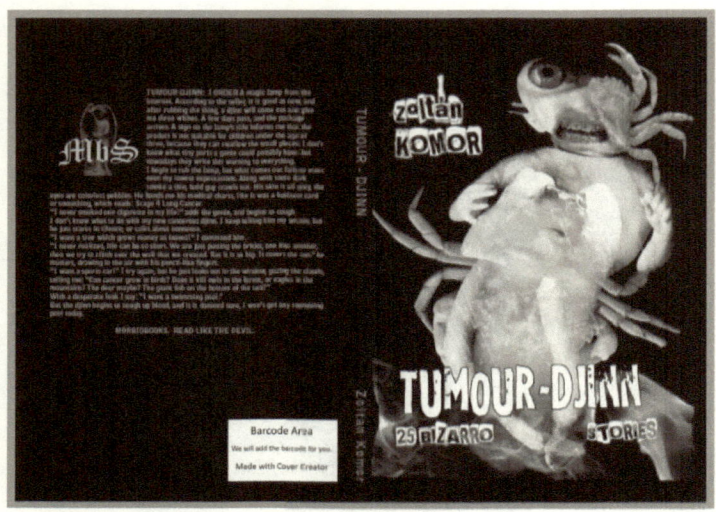

~I ORDER A magic lamp from the internet. According to the
seller, it is good as new, and after rubbing the thing, a djinn
will come out and give me three wishes. I begin to rub the
lamp. Along with some dark smoke a thin, bald guy crawls out.
His skin is all grey, the eyes are colorless pebbles.

"I want a tree which grows money as leaves!" I command.

"I never realized life can be so short. We are just putting the
bricks, one into another, and then we try to climb over the wall
that we created. But it is so big. It covers the sun." he mutters.

"I want a sports car!" I try again, but he just looks out in the
window, gazing the clouds, telling me: "Can cancer grow in
birds? Does it kill owls in the forest, or eagles in the
mountains? The deer maybe? The giant fish on the bottom of
the sea?"

With a desperate look I say: 'I want a swimming pool."

But the djinn begins to cough up blood, and it is damned sure,
I won't get any swimming pool today.

Gregor

~**Keegan is a late-night public access radio show host,** sexual deviant, and militant vegan. He has grown tired of his vegan cause being treated with apathy by the portly, meat-gorging, residents of the small town of Breen Gay, Wisconsin.

The time is ripe for Vegan vengeance.

Keegan harvests roundworms from a local vagrant and mutates them using chemicals stolen from the meat packing plant. He infests the populace with the voracious, parasitic carnivores. Keegan knows that the only way for the people of Breen Gay to eliminate the parasites is to starve them of meat. It is with great expectation that he awaits the oncoming utopia of Veganism.

However, the mutant roundworms will not die easily. The problems for the people of Breen Gay have only just begun.

~FOR SO LONG as anyone could remember, The Flagrant Five have ruled the land with an aggressive hand—enslaving children, destroying the wilderness—but Father Necrocious is tired of it all. One of his worst enemies (and a member of the Flagrant Five), Manservant Genesis, has escaped his imprisonment as a shadow. Therefore, he's enlisted the help of a ragtag group of fabricated Mercenaries to turn the fascists to shadows. The annual Dictators' Ball is pending (a battle in which children are used as pawns to determine the fate of the free world), and the brothers plan to stop the gala before it can commence. As they weave their way through the cartoonish landscape they will fight with their options to either trap the Flagrant Five with their shadow guns, or disobey their creator's orders and finally kill the Five for good.

~**The hands of the girls were inside of each-others zip front grey boiler suits** and they sat in the blood from where Sonny's face collided with the surface. The brunette had a finger smear of it next to her mouth.

"You two sluts put each other down and go tell Moira that Sonny's done. I'm coming in, just got a little business to attend to first."

As the two started to leave the big blond grabbed the shoulder of the red head and pulled her back.

"Not you Fire-Crotch, all this fucking blood has got me going." She started to unbuckle the belt on her camouflage hot pants. "Down you go, bitch!"

~**Short stories from the Most Depraved Writer in Print.** Dark and twisted tales of exquisite violence, rough tricks, narcotics consumption, evil ghosts and drug-snuffling demons. Evil grandfathers and animal-human hybrid clones. Morbid serial killer stalking night darkened hallways of an unsuspecting hospital. Life underground following the frozen apocalypse. Tales of ancient blood-thirsty vampires and Roman decadence. Enjoy all of the hardcore, dystopic, viscerally violent stories. Not for easily offended mamby-pambies. Dark fiction at its finest.

Gregor

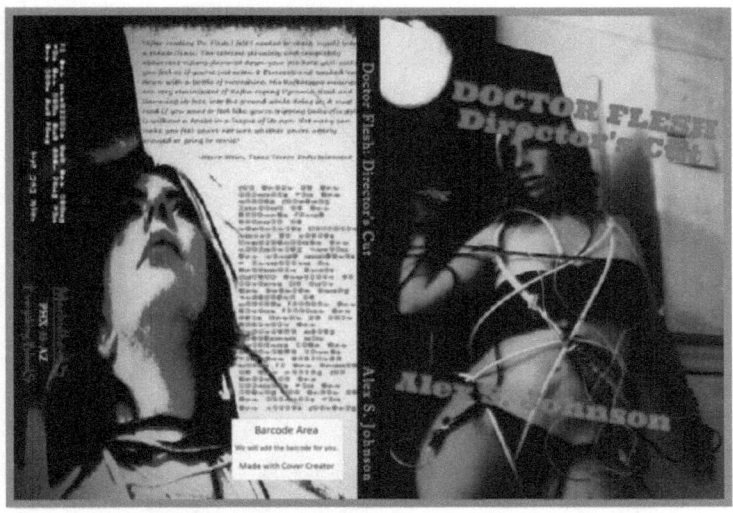

~From Alex S. Johnson, the author of Bad Sunset, Wicked Candy and The Death Jazz, comes a new vision in Bizarro horror. Imagine a TROMA film on meth and acid, one part cyberpunk, one part Franz Kafka, and three parts frankly unsuitable for a sane audience. "Will make you feel as if you've just eaten 8 Percocets and washed 'em down with a bottle of moonshine," says Necro Stein of Texas Terror Entertainment.

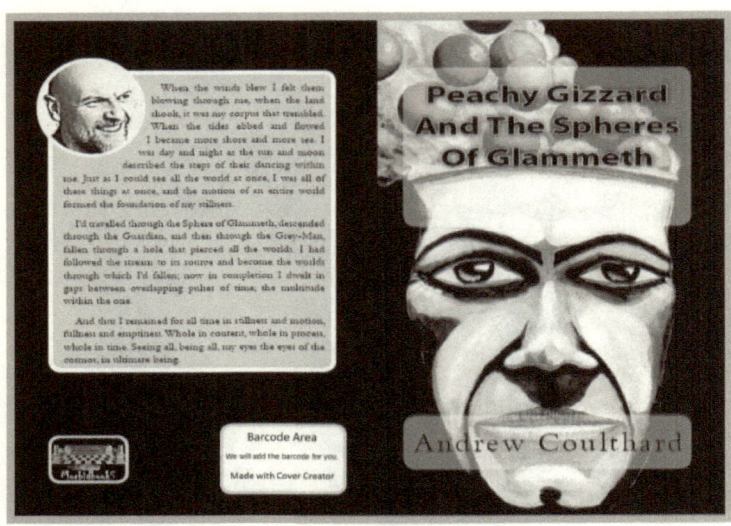

~**When the winds blew i felt them blowing through me,** when the land shook, it was my corpus that trembled. When the tides ebbed and flowed I became more shore and more sea. I was day and night as the sun and moon described the steps of their dancing within me. Just as I could see all the world at once, I was all of these things at once, and the motion of an entire world formed the foundation of my stillness.

I'd travelled through the Sphere of Glammeth, descended through the Guardian, and then through the Grey-Man, fallen through a hole that pierced all the worlds.

Gregor

~**He had to have her the moment he saw her trachea ring.** Six months later she was his lovely wife. He performed his duties as a husband and she as a wife. He tolerated a house filled with references to her late first husband and the children they had together. He put up with her prudish ways. He waited. He was patient. He planned. He was adaptable. He was rewarded over the course of a week in her basement. He turned his perverse sexual fantasies of worms and maggots and her lovely crusty trachea ring into a gruesome reality.

~A dirty shameful devil of a secret...

Something that two men share. A legacy that will shock you to your very core. One that is created not out of madness, but of the purest desire. Take a vivid journey into the mind of the killer and his biggest fan. Do you believe in evil? See the knife plunge. Lap at the wounds. Do you still? There is no rational meaning or pretty words that will hide away the darkness that the words of this found journal creates. Inside is the real truth. And it can set you free. Watch all you want. Taste what you dare not have.

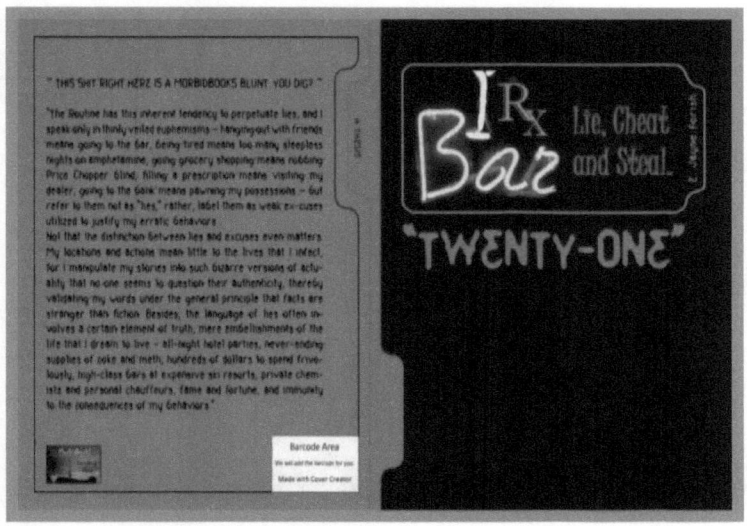

~"**The routine has this inherent tendency to perpetuate lies,** and I speak only in thinly veiled euphemisms — hanging out with friends means going to the bar; being tired means too many sleepless nights on amphetamine; going grocery shopping means robbing Price Chopper blind; filling a prescription means visiting my dealer; going to the bank means pawning my possessions — but refer to them not as "lies;" rather, label them as weak excuses utilized to justify my erratic behaviours.

~**I'm feeling down and dirty, feeling kind of mean,** so I give those fans my middle finger. Those poor bastards go nuts. My team looks at me in awe. My coach frowns and the opposing one begins to furiously scratch out new plays. I see our opponents and I almost feel sorry for the poor bastards. Their fans can't help them. Their coach can't help them. I'm going to run them off their own track in front of their own fans and there is not one thing they can do about it.

Gregor

~Humanity is the devil is a deconstructed nightmare mixing David Lynch and snuff movies. The plot revolves around a central character, Seth, who is set about a crusade against humanity which, for him, represents pure evil. Through random killings he and his cronies try to accelerate the end of the world, in order to provoke and defeat the Demiurge, the false God that is ruling the earth. As in Burroughs, logical language is replaced here with cut-scenes – sometimes to be taken literally – that plunge the reader into an extreme experience.

Cole

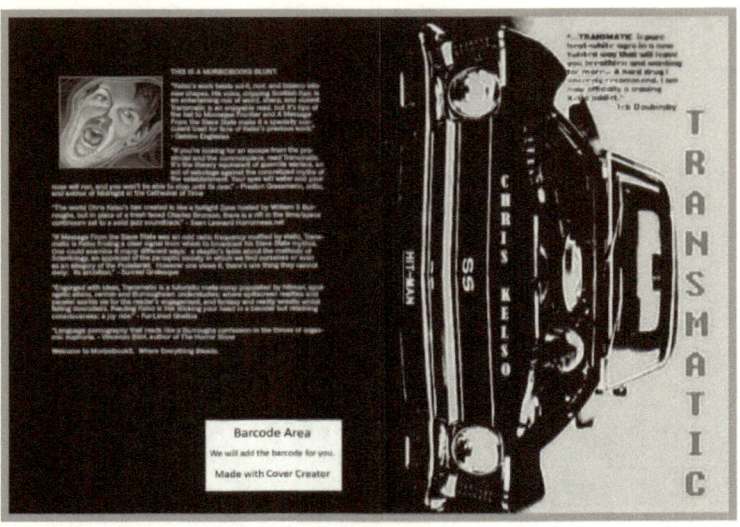

~"As a part-time hitman/ exterminator, Ignius Ellis's dream is to buy a candy-apple red Nova Supreme. In the process of trying to earn enough cash to make his dream come true he gets sucked into the rough world of Visitacion Valley, SF. When the tenants in his apartment complex reveal their various extracurricular activities this take an even more bizarre twist and Ellis soon becomes acquainted with the nightmarish Slave State dimension..."

~That's the last time she gets the bigger worm...

Once their flesh flakes away the angels collapse into puddles of hissing goop and withered petals blow into them hurried along by unseen winds. My spit looses its sweet taste to the black flavor of ash. The glowing birds in the bright orange sky burst into small sparkly novas. The sky itself weeps and tears, streaking down like a ruined painting as the dismal grey of life wheezes back before my eyes. I don't blink; praying silently for one last desperate sensation of the high. Lila feels it too. She writhes on the mattress next to me…

~Scary as ever.

He looked at her and grinned wickedly, the overcasting shadows of the outer corner of the stone wall, combined with the flickering light above them, created a deadly feature across the side of his face. He sees her lying helpless. He chuckled eerily, and instantly raised his hand. Her eyes widened to the sight of the gleaming sharp knife in his grasp. He even held it up for her to see it better.

She stared up at him and then to the knife, panting in fear. Her heart pounded throughout her body as he chuckled once more saying deeply,

"Oh excellent. I've found you . . ."

Gregor

~**Within these twisted and perverted pages**, Johnson manages to demolish clichés with a jaded finesse that I've personally never encountered in written form. Another apparent talent is his effortless deconstruction of pop-culture allegories and references as found in his story "Vampussy." No one is safe or spared from his dagger sharp sarcasm and wit.

While not without its flaws, my appreciation for this kind of talent and voice is what made his writing so fun to read, even if he might possibly be out of his ever-loving mind.

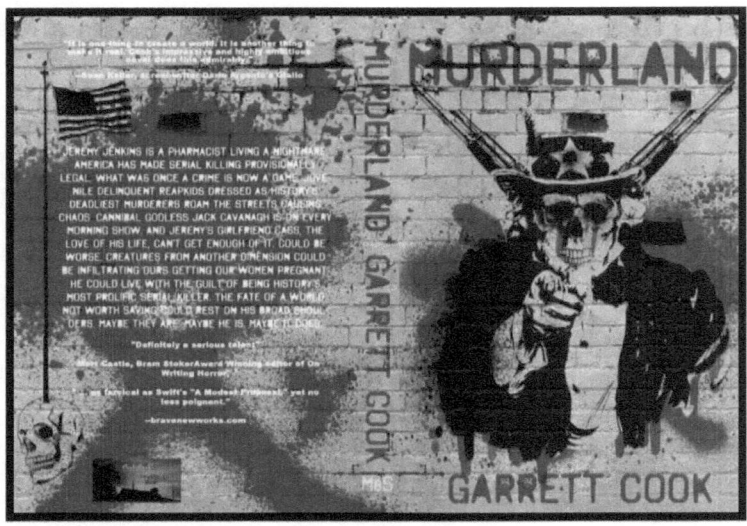

~In Garrett Cook's Murderland serial killers are idolized by society. Their deeds are followed obsessively by television pundits and the adoring public. A subculture has grown up around this phenomena, called "Reap." Laws are created to allow this activity to flourish, including designated "safe zones' where killers can practice their trade without fear of persecution. Fans of the top rated serial killers celebrate each new kill on social media and television. Programs glorify their deeds.

The culture of Murderland is violent and mirrors our own violent society and its decadent obsessions.

~Born whole from the rectum of a dying patient, Morbid silently stalks the hospital's hallways, heinously dispatching the most helpless of patients and in the most painfully repulsive of manners. In the meantime, in order to pay for his family and home that includes his ghost step-father Sammy and his pet aborted fetus Chip, Westphal has to ingest mounds of dangerous narcotics to get through his night shifts. Barely hanging on to his Care Tech gig by his fingernails, the last thing Westphal needs is to be accused of Morbid's evil deeds. You, on the other hand, simply seek some solace from all Your diseases.

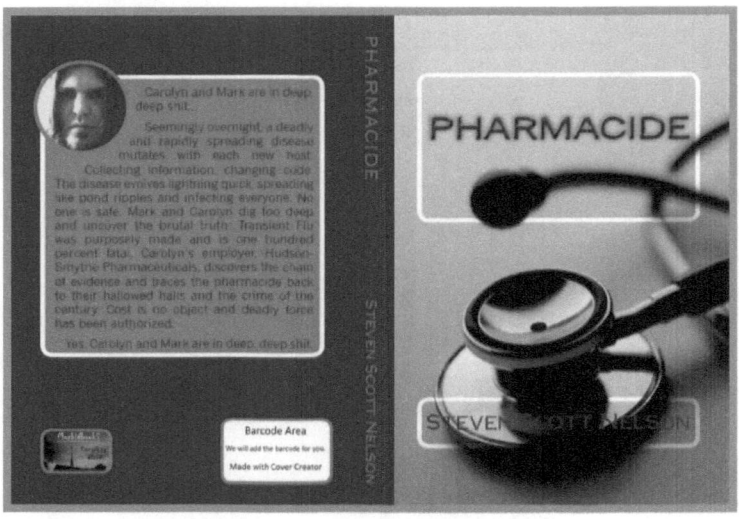

~It looks like Carolyn and Mark are in deep, deep shit... Mark and Carolyn live in an alternate 1989 where Ronald Reagan is on his fourth presidential term. The USA has a rigid, long-standing caste system and abortions were never made legal. Being homeless is a crime that is punishable by imprisonment in Tent City. Most of Mark's ER patients are inmates at this camp and are victims of a new disease dubbed, Transient Flu. This deadly and rapidly spreading disease mutates with each new host, collecting information, changing code. The disease evolves lightning quick, spreading like pond ripples...

Gregor

~IMMANUEL THE CHRIST has some nerve. Jonah has already lost everyone he loves to Pilate the vampire and his Harbor drug violence. Jonah now trudges through his days staying as high on Plata as possible. He just wants to be left alone while he waits for his turn to die. The Christ has other plans for him. She sends Pedro, to assign Jonah to order the Herod to dismantle the Harbor's Plata trade. Jonah decides to run. But you can't run from God. As Jonah learns the hard way when the 'Edmund Fitzgerald' goes down in rough seas, with the reluctant prophet on board…

~**Five Very Wicked Shorts**. Brought to you with love and blood from The Grim Reverend Steven Rage, the 'Most Depraved Writer in Print'. ~

Through the sheer shock of his presentation, Rage forces readers to consider the alternatives, to look at the garbage in the streets, to see what is swept into the gutters at night right before all decent people awake to see another cleaned up version of the day. Depravity at its finest, but really the stories are loads of fun.

~**Pontius Pilate is cursed to be a vampire.** Life after life after life.~ And for the Plata dealing Pilate, his life is more like a death sentence. His only chance surviving is to keep on selling his monthly quota of Plata. This new man-made narcotic is a potent speed-ball designed to amp up the user, while also numbing the conscience into euphoric oblivion. To nullify the pain. To stifle the torture. To run and to hid from all the anguish inside. PILATE is a drug lord vampire in this re-telling of Christ's final days.

~So I, The Spun Monkey, have returned from running my errands, safe and sound. Having failed rehab once again, The Spun Monkey went ahead and procured myself an 8-ball of crispy, crunchy Columbian Bam-Bam. I chipped, chopped, lined and blasted off with two bigguns up each side. OOH OOH EEE EEE-fuckmerunning- OOH-OOH-OOH, motherfuckers! Monkey be ready... Yes, indeeeeeed.... Having had my jet fuel, I then sat my hairy asshole down at the keyboard and began flailing away. The monkey hopes you dig the fruits of my labors in 'The Spun Monkey's Digest'. And if you not ... well then ... you can go eff yourself, Capitan!

~**Following religious folklore, parables, and beliefs,** Rage presents the readers with a God who truly is the Shepherd that leaves no sheep behind. While this tale is deeply woven with the intricacies of a dark, drug-infested world ruled by evil forces, this is the story of a lost sheep. All are God's children, even the most foulest of evil creatures who by their own will have become so through their spiritual and physical copulation with the Devil, and as such, in God's mercy, still are given a chance to be saved.

~ CARGO CONTAINS:

1. *Space-wrecked on Venus* by NEIL R. JONES
2. *For All the Marbles* by REV. STEVEN RAGE
3. *Tony and the Beetles* by PHILIP K. DICK
4. *Acid Bath* by VASELEOS GARSON
5. *The Butterfly Kiss* by ARTHUR DEKKER SAVAGE
6. *The Moon Destroyers* by MONROE K. RUCH

FROM SOME OF THE GIANTS OF THE GOLDEN AGE to the darkest of dystopian noir, MorbidbookS SciFi Anthology will take you from hopeful space travel to living hand-to-mouth in the despair beneath the Earth.
Welcome to your future.

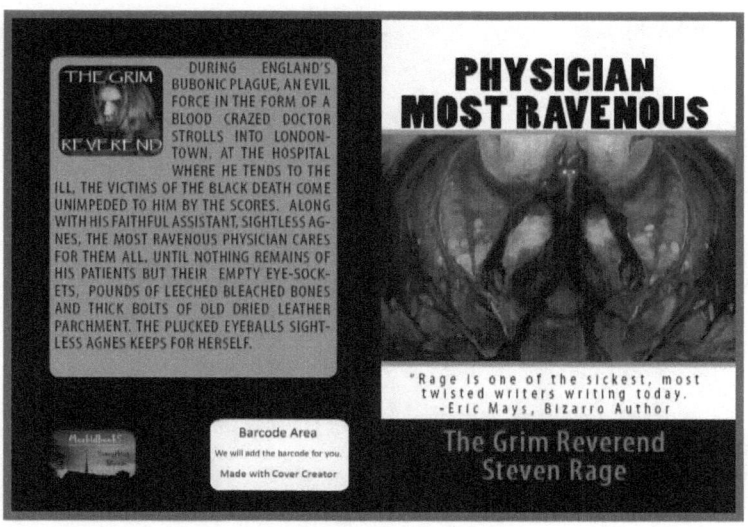

~During the height of England's Bubonic Plague an ancient
Evil Force strolls into London-Town in the form of a would-be
doctor. It could smell the blood from miles away, wanting only
to help. At the hospital where he cares for the victims of this
Black Death, the ill come to him unimpeded. They arrived and
fell by the scores. With the help of his ever-faithful assistant,
Sightless Agnes, a most ravenous cares for them all. Eating his
way through an entire hospital, he treats them until there is
nothing left. Nothing save their empty eye sockets, a few
pounds of leeched bleached bones and some bolts of old dried-
out flesh-leather parchment.

~New from MorbidbookS: Where Everything Bleeds is an instant collector's specimen and a certain stunner. ~ Be the first freak on your block to acquire this singular and unexpurgated exquisite culling of The Grim Reverend Steven Rage's favorite 'meds'. Enjoy this one-of-a-kind vivid look into the twisted mind of The Most Depraved Writer In Print as he captains you through the intoxicating stain of his wicked imagination. Included are numerous Photos, Paintings and Illustrations embellished with dramatic grayscale that enhance these iniquitous and magnificent Dark Fantasy fables.